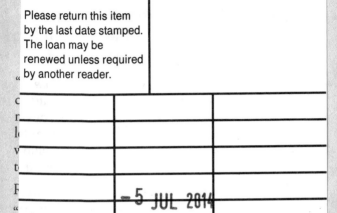
c
r
l
v
t
F
"
v
g
H
g
"
"
e
F
o

V
in
h

to know exactly wha
response ou
to caress he
to bring he

Books by Lisa Watson

Harlequin Kimani Romance

Love Contract
Her Heart's Desire

LISA WATSON

is native of Washington D.C., and the city's historic and political backdrop fed her romantic imagination. Her hobbies are as eclectic as her music collection, but what Lisa loves the most is writing strong, positive characters who are memorable to the reader and fun. The picturesque locales Lisa visits always seem to find a way into her latest novels. Lisa has been married for sixteen years and lives in the Raleigh, NC, area with her husband, two teenagers and Maltipoo, Brinkley.

Want to connect with Lisa? Contact her at lywatson007@hotmail.com, on Facebook (NCLisaWatson) or Twitter (@lywatson007).

Her HEART'S Desire

LISA WATSON

H HARLEQUIN® KIMANI™ ROMANCE

To C. Adele Dodson. My Aunt…My Friend.

Recycling programs
for this product may
not exist in your area.

ISBN-13: 978-0-373-86356-3

HER HEART'S DESIRE

Copyright © 2014 by Lisa Y. Watson

HARLEQUIN®

Printed in U.S.A.

™ www.Harlequin.com

Dear Reader,

When it comes to hitting the mark with love, both Tiffany Gentry and Lt. Colonel Ivan Mangum have their share of misses. For both, past experiences have shaped them and caused hurdles to overcome as they navigate their way to true love. Norma Jean Anderson, aka the Love Broker, makes Tiffany her "love" project this time, dispensing sage advice on finding lasting happiness. A boutique owner, Tiffany is fiercely independent, which Ivan appreciates, but causes some contention for the overly protective man of action. I love these characters and their supporting cast. For this couple, the road to compromise is not always a smooth one. Can they find commonality, or will differing opinions tear them apart?

I hope you enjoy this Harlequin Kimani Romance book. I'm currently writing the final story in The Match Broker series. Keep reading to find out who's next on Norma Jean's radar!

Be Inspired…

Lisa

Acknowledgments

It's amazing how many lasting friendships I've acquired by attending both the Romance Slam Jam and RT Booklovers Convention. Many of my opportunities and connections simply would not have been if it weren't for the incredible people associated with these events. A special thank you to *RT Book Reviews* founder Kathryn Falk, president Ken Rubin and editor Carol Stacy for memories, friendships and learning that will last a lifetime!

My thanks to Pat Simmons, fellow author, confidant, critique buddy and overall wonderful person! Your unconditional love and advice are invaluable. Thanks for the many, many phone calls over the years to keep me and my characters on track!

To Tina Ezell Hull, another amazing writer and phenomenal woman! You keep me laughing, crying and eternally grateful for taking a ladies' room break! I love you and those original, and poignant, Southern Belle tales!

To Renee Bernard, the newest member of my lifetime friend group and an extraordinary writer. I believe Leslie brought us together, and in a ladies' room, no less! Our connection was instant, and our friendship sealed with laughter, tears, wine and love! What more could I ask for!? And thank you so much for The Jaded!

To my rocks: My husband, Eric, my unbelievably talented teens, Brandon and Alyssa, and my mother, siblings and family. Your love, support and understanding make it possible for me to live my dream!

For my readers—your kind words, love of my stories, support and excitement are what keep me going. Onward and upward!

Chapter 1

An impeccably dressed man stood across the glass countertop that separated Tiffany Gentry from her customers. Before she could offer him help, the gentleman interrupted.

"I've got to say you're so gorgeous your beauty is hurting my eyes."

That's the best he's got? Tiffany plastered a smile of thanks on her face when she wanted to smirk. The corny come-on lines were getting tiresome, but he was her customer, and a sale was a sale.

"Then perhaps I should step away while you pick out a necklace? I wouldn't want to eclipse it with my beauty."

He laughed loudly before looking at her again. "I love women with spunk. I doubt I'll find anything as delightful as you, but I'll try."

The front door chimed, interrupting their conversation, for which Tiffany was grateful.

"Welcome to the Petite Boutique, I'll be with you in a moment," she said without looking up.

Her attention was still on the undecided flirt. Now he was leaning so far over the display case that his breath steamed up the glass.

The man sighed aloud. "Yes indeed, with so many choices, I can't decide."

Tiffany glanced toward the front of the store. She spotted a tall man looking at a display. Excusing herself, she walked over to him.

"Good morning, are you looking for something specific?"

"Yes," he said, turning around to face her. "The owner."

Tiffany stared at him. He was much taller up close, well built and had just done a marvelous job of rendering her speechless. She stood there staring so long that he finally said, "Do you know where I can find her?"

"Oh," she croaked, extending her hand. "I'm me...that would be me...Tiffany Gentry. How can I help you?"

"I'm here to help you," he replied, closing his fingers around hers in a firm shake.

There were a number of possibilities that sprang to mind on how he could help. The first was to help her up after she collapsed in a pool of hormones on her polished wooden floor.

"I'm sorry. I guess I should introduce myself. Colonel Ivan Mangum," he said with a slight smile.

"It's a pleasure to meet you, Colonel," she replied warmly. Her skin tingled at the contact. She loved men with solid handshakes—no spaghetti hands. To Tiffany, firm grips exuded confidence and strength. "You know, when I called a few days ago, I had no idea you'd be able to give me an evaluation this fast."

"Ms. Jeannie stressed that you needed something in place right away."

"Sooner rather than later would be best. I've got to say, Ms. Jeannie thinks highly of you. She wouldn't take no for an answer and practically hovered over me while I dialed your number."

A rumble of laughter escaped his lips. "I understand, and yes, Ms. Jeannie can be persuasive."

Relief swept over her face. "She can indeed."

When Norma Jean Anderson, Tiffany's friend Milán's mother-in-law, had mentioned she knew someone who could help, Tiffany agreed that her safety and that of the store should be her priority.

Norma Jean had told her about a man who used to be in the army, owned his own business and had installed the security system at the senior center where she taught fitness classes. Now here he was, walking around inspecting her boutique with a practiced eye. Tiffany couldn't help but feel protective of her shop while it was raked over by his penetrating stare.

"This is an eclectic store."

"Isn't it?" Tiffany said. "There's something for everyone. Most items are one of a kind. We carry jewelry that I make myself, and I've got some artisan friends whose work I showcase, too. They make T-shirts, soaps, lotions and even pottery."

Ivan looked around again appreciatively. "How many rooms do you have?"

"I've got the main area here, a storage room and bathroom. There's an exit from the storage room. That's where I receive larger deliveries."

He nodded and typed some notes on his laptop. "When I first spoke to Ms. Jeannie, she told me that you'd had a break-in a few weeks ago?"

"It wasn't exactly a break-in. More like an overzealous customer who wouldn't leave. I didn't hear him come in."

"A forced entry?"

"No. I was closed for the night. The door was unlocked,

which was my fault. The chime didn't go off. When I came out, there he was."

"Did you call the police and fill out a report? Did they dust for fingerprints?"

She shook her head. "He didn't take anything, and I got him to leave so I didn't call, but it was still…"

Ivan looked down when she stopped talking. "Unsettling?"

Tiffany glanced up at him. His matter-of-fact expression from seconds earlier was replaced with one of concern. There was something about his relaxed manner that made her feel better.

"Yes. I've taken a self-defense class. I'm an only child. I'm used to dealing with problems myself, but in that moment, I wondered if I could remember what I'd been taught. Could I protect myself?"

Before Ivan could reply, the man across the room cleared his throat loudly.

Tiffany gazed over her shoulder. "I should get back to my customer."

Ivan gave her a reassuring smile. "I'm going to take some measurements and continue looking around if that's okay?"

"Of course."

Shortly afterward, the man strode out of the store in a huff. Tiffany was pretty good at reading customers. Her intuition told her he wanted to play, not buy.

Without customers, Tiffany focused on Ivan. When Norma Jean said he used to be a colonel in the army, she'd pictured a stodgy old white-haired man with a thickening midsection. Tiffany was wrong. She wondered if Ivan had been to exotic places all over the world, spoke several languages and was an expert in lethal weapons. Granted, she may be dramatizing his abilities based on some of her favorite television shows, but he looked capable.

What a magnificent body. At five feet two and a half inches, it was a given that most people were taller than her, but she guessed he was at least six-two or six-three. His job certainly kept him in shape. His dark suit and French Blue shirt fit like they were tailored. With his physique, he could easily have stepped off the cover of a *Men's Health* magazine.

Ivan had flawless light brown skin, except for a small scar on the right side of his jaw. His eyes were a vivid amber-brown, which was a sharp contrast to his thick dark eyebrows and lashes. Dark hair cut close made her wonder what it would feel like to run the palm of her hand down the smooth nape of his neck. The urge to do it made her fingers tingle.

You've just met him, and you're drooling over the man. But he was charismatic, and droolworthy.

She turned to see Ivan leaning on the wall opposite the counter with an amused look on his rugged face. "Have you finished?" she asked him.

"I have." Ivan sauntered toward her. "The only thing older than that security system is the building itself."

Tiffany laughed. "You're right. I inherited it when I bought the place. The alarm is temperamental, and works when it wants to—like my last sales associate. Truthfully, I haven't given it another thought until now."

"Were you thinking the standard motion sensors with delayed-entry keypad, or something more advanced like heat signature, night-vision cameras and—"

"Whoa," she cut him off. "Nothing too advanced. With my budget, I can't afford *Mission: Impossible*–type security. I need a modest security system where I can enter a code, turn it on or off—and a panic button, of course."

"Of course. You'll also want a monitoring agency to alert the police?"

"Sounds good to me."

He made a few more notes before asking, "Will other companies be bidding?"

"I'd say that depends on you, Colonel Mangum."

"Call me Ivan. I appreciate the opportunity, and I'm sure I can help. I'll call you when I have the proposal ready." He extended his hand. "A pleasure, Miss Gentry."

"Tiffany," she corrected. Her hand slid into his. "Likewise."

After he left, Tiffany went to the storage room to get a box of clothing. She placed it on the counter, pulled up a stool and began to add price tags. While she worked, she made a mental note to thank Norma Jean for recommending Ivan. He'd been a pleasant diversion today.

The phone's ring startled her from thoughts of Ivan Mangum.

"Thank you for calling the Petite Boutique. How may I help you?"

"How did it go?" Milán Anderson, Tiffany's best friend, asked. "Was the guy competent?"

"Yes." Tiffany leaned against the counter. "Not what I expected."

"Uh-oh," her friend said with concern. "Good or bad?"

A smile covered Tiffany's face. "Fantastic. I expected some old boring guy with a large belly."

"Was he?"

"Nope." Tiffany sighed. "Lani, he was straight out of an action movie—tall, commanding and built like he's been working out since childhood."

"What a meeting. Was business discussed, or did you drool the whole time?"

"It was all business. He's probably married or has a girlfriend."

Tiffany filled Milán in on her appointment with Ivan, then they hung up.

A healthy appreciation for a gorgeous man was fine, but

she would not act on her impulses. She had been attracted to one too many men who were unavailable, and for all she knew, he was just the same. Still, it was impossible not to be drawn to him. When it came to first impressions, Colonel Ivan Mangum was definitely an Army of One.

Chapter 2

Tiffany almost dropped a glass bowl she was wrapping in tissue paper a few days later when Ivan walked in. He was wearing a pair of jeans, and a dark gray Under Armour shirt that fit him like a second skin.

She walked up to him as he was eyeing a crystal owl pendant. "Wow, you have my quote already?"

Ivan grinned. "Soon."

"Did you have more questions?"

"Not on security. I've got a dilemma and thought you could help."

"Of course. What's the problem?"

"I need a gift. My grandmother turns ninety-six next week."

Tiffany relaxed. "You've come to the right place. What does your grandmother like? Does she have any hobbies?"

As they discussed his grandmother, Tiffany guided Ivan around the store, showing him everything from velvet wraps to ceramic bowls, but nothing seemed right.

"Wait, I've got it." With a grin, she retrieved the owl pendant and held it out to him. "It caught your eye earlier, and from what you've told me about her, I think she would love having something almost as wise as she is."

Ivan's fingers connected with hers. His touch was warm as it grazed her palm. He tilted the pendant in the light.

"That's true. Always go with your gut, right?"

She laughed. "Words I live by."

"In that case, I'll take it."

"Wise choice." Tiffany winked. "I'll wrap it for you."

Celeste, one of Tiffany's employees, rang up Ivan's purchase while she wrapped the gift with care. Tiffany placed the birthday gift in a decorative bag and handed it to Ivan.

"I hope she loves it."

"I'll let you know. Thanks for coming to my rescue."

A warm smile brightened her face. "Anytime."

For the second time that week, Tiffany found herself staring as he walked out of the store.

The phone rang, causing Tiffany to almost jump out of her skin. She picked it up.

"Hi, honey. You're not busy, are you?"

"No, Ms. Jeannie. What's up?"

"I wanted to make sure you're coming to the party tonight."

"Like I would miss Milán and Adrian's anniversary party. Of course I'll be there," Tiffany said.

"Great. Are you bringing a date? If you're not, I've got a few prospects."

Sometimes Norma Jean was overzealous in her matchmaking quest. And it seemed it was too late to dissuade her now.

"Ms. Jeannie," Tiffany began, "I appreciate what you're trying to do, but—"

"Trust me, dear. It'll work out great. I promise. Now don't be late."

Before Tiffany could say another word, Norma Jean had hung up.

A blind date was the last thing on her mind, but getting that point across to Norma Jean was more impossible than keeping shoppers orderly at a Bath & Body Works semiannual sale.

Ivan opened the door to his parents' two-story home and flipped the light on. He juggled car keys, his grandmother's gift and a large brown paper bag. Kicking the door shut with his foot, Ivan set everything but the bag on the hall table.

"I'm home," he called out.

"Down in a minute," his brother replied from upstairs.

He went in the kitchen for plates, silverware and beers. Back on the couch, he took his carryout dinner out of its bag and assembled his meal.

Cole Mangum walked into the room. "Hey." He picked up the remote and turned the television on before sitting next to his brother.

"Hey, yourself."

"It's Friday night," Cole pointed out.

"Yeah, and?"

"What are you doing home?"

"Cole, I'm home every night," his brother replied in a dry tone. "What are *you* doing home?"

"Waiting to see what's for dinner," he joked.

"Thai food," Ivan replied, while dumping a mound of shrimp pad thai onto his plate. "I got your favorite."

"Cool, thanks."

Cole picked up a plate and helped himself to red curry with chicken. He strategically spooned it over his brown rice.

They ate in silence until Cole asked, "How's work

going? It's been a few weeks since you've had an assignment. Aren't you getting restless?"

"No. Helping people out while I'm here has kept me busy. In fact, I'm working on an alarm system now for a small boutique owner, Tiffany Gentry. I'll need your help on it, by the way."

"Is she the one Mrs. Anderson told you about?"

"Yes."

"Is she attractive?"

Ivan stopped chewing. "Cole."

A wide grin etched his brother's face. "What? I'm just asking."

"She's a client," Ivan dismissed.

"So? That time in Munich—"

"Drop it."

Cole glanced at his brother. "What's the big deal? What she looks like isn't classified information."

Ivan took a sip of his beer. "She's about five foot three inches tall, has bright, expressive brown eyes, dark hair with highlights that she wears spiked and beautiful mocha skin. She has a beauty mole above her right collarbone, and when she smiles…her whole face lights up. She's left-handed, sure of herself and wears a floral fragrance that reminds me of the ocean. It suits her."

Cole tried not to laugh. "Did you miss anything?"

"In my line of work, it's imperative to assess problems quickly—and people."

"I don't doubt it. She sounds like a beautiful woman."

Ivan didn't like where the conversation was going one bit. "Don't even think about it, baby brother."

"No reason why both of us should miss out," Cole reasoned.

Before Ivan could open his mouth, Cole burst into laughter.

"Dude, I'm kidding. Don't get worked up."

Ivan's eyebrow shot upward. "You haven't seen me worked up."

Cole sat back and put his feet up. "I'm sure that's true, Colonel Mangum."

An hour of dinner and television later, Ivan stood up. "I've got some work to do."

Cole glanced at him. "Go ahead, I'll clean up."

Ivan thanked him and headed upstairs. He retrieved his laptop and sat down on the couch in his sitting area. He placed his feet on an old leather trunk and got to work on Tiffany's proposal.

But twenty minutes later, he found himself leaning back, closing his eyes and recalling his initial meeting with Tiffany. Her playful manner and humor were refreshing. In his line of work, a personal life was challenging. Working in the private sector was no different. Ivan's company and his time centered on his clients. Some of his men and women traveled to dangerous locations with dignitaries, business professionals and wealthy notables.

Even when he wasn't on assignment, Ivan was involved in each case to ensure the safety of his employees and customers. The hours were long and the job physically demanding, but he was proud of his accomplishments and thriving business. He excelled at it, and loved every minute.

A knock sounded at his bedroom door, and Cole entered.

"Mom called. She asked how the renovations were going, and if we were eating."

Ivan shook his head and smiled. His mother was a worrier. It had been eight months since he'd moved back to his family's home in the Beverly neighborhood of Chicago. With work keeping him busy, he had taken his parents, Lennox and Maris, up on their offer to move back home and make Chicago his hub. Since they now spent the winter months in St. John, that gave him and Cole time to reconnect. So far they were making the most of their temporary bachelor pad.

"Did you tell her that you haven't cooked since they left?"

"Ha. I told her we're doing well, and the guest bathroom is coming along. She wants us to send some pics."

Thanks to their father, Ivan and Cole were pretty handy carpenters. While their parents were gone, the brothers had decided to upgrade the first-floor bathroom. The remodel, his business and checking on their grandmother, Cecile Mangum, kept him busy. GiGi, as he and Cole called her, lived in an assisted-living facility in nearby Evanston. As the oldest, it was his duty to keep his feisty grandmother and Cole out of trouble while his parents were gone. It was a full-time job.

Cole sat down and propped up his feet on Ivan's trunk. "Did you finish your proposal?"

"Not yet. I got…sidetracked."

"What's the cause of your preoccupation—or who?"

Ivan remained silent.

"Come on, Ivan. I can tell you like her."

"Sure I do. Tiffany is a likable woman."

"That's not what I mean, and you know it. It's written all over that stern face of yours. You're attracted to her."

"I've got work to do, Cole," Ivan said.

Cole stood up. "Fine. I guess I'll let you get back to it, then."

"Good. I'll see you later."

After his brother left, Ivan resumed working. He was diligent for a while, but his attention kept straying to Tiffany. She was unlike any woman he knew. Her sense of humor made him smile, and her beauty and spirit appealed to him.

But Cole's reference to Munich was a somber reminder not to get involved with clients. The Munich incident had involved a friend of a client. When it was time for him to leave, she had not taken the news well. That had caused animosity from his client, and Ivan had vowed to keep things strictly professional after that.

Standing up suddenly, Ivan decided to go for a run. Physical exertion would get Tiffany Gentry off his mind— and if it didn't, he was in trouble.

Big trouble.

Chapter 3

The party was at MG restaurant in a private dining room on the second floor. It was sophisticated and quiet, with perfect views of the Magnificent Mile. It was a fitting backdrop to celebrate her best friend's first wedding anniversary. Tiffany set her gift on a beautifully decorated table, then walked over to hug Adrian's mother.

"How are you, Ms. Jeannie? The room is amazing."

Norma Jean Anderson beamed with pride. "Honey, they've outdone themselves," she replied, hooking her arm through Tiffany's. "I couldn't be more pleased. This is the first restaurant they dined at after returning from their honeymoon. I thought it a fitting place for the newlyweds to celebrate their first year together."

"I agree. You look beautiful, too."

Norma Jean's silver cowl-necked gown shimmered on her slender body and complemented her honey-toned complexion. Her gray hair was cut short in a style that suited her no-nonsense personality and classic elegance.

"Thank you, dear. You look divine in that dress of yours. Good thing there'll be plenty of single men at this party like I promised." Norma Jean nudged Tiffany.

"About that, Ms. Jeannie," Tiffany began.

"Speaking of single men, did you call Colonel Mangum?"

"I did," Tiffany replied. "He came out to the shop today and looked around."

"He did?" Norma Jean replied. "And?"

"And he said he'd give me a quote in a few days."

Norma Jean leaned closer to Tiffany. "Ivan is such a sweet man. Why he's still single is anyone's guess."

Tiffany ignored that remark. Luckily Heathcliffe Anderson came up behind his wife just then. He greeted Tiffany and placed an arm around Norma Jean.

Norma Jean kissed Tiffany's cheek and then turned to her husband. "Cliff, don't just stand there, go alert the photographer that Adrian and Milán are here while I get the group in position."

Her husband shook his head and leaned down and whispered conspiratorially in Tiffany's ear, "Jeannie told me I didn't have to do any work for this shindig, but we see how that turned out." With a wink, he headed off to complete his assignment.

Tiffany hoped that when she got to be Ms. Jeannie's age, she and her husband would tease each other like that. *If* she were married, that is. Up to this point, not one marriage in her family could be considered a testament to happily-ever-after. Her parents had divorced when she was fifteen, and were cordial when forced to be in close proximity. But the tension was always thick enough to cut. The other relatives that stayed married were so miserable, they would have been better off going their separate ways.

Tiffany was talking with friends when Mr. and Mrs. Adrian Anderson entered. The crowd applauded and cheered as the two made their way to the center of the room. After welcoming the guests and toasting the happy couple, Norma Jean turned the floor over to Milán and Adrian. After all the speeches were finished, Tiffany went over to her best friend, and the two women embraced.

"You look amazing," Tiffany said.

"Gracias. Tú también," Milán replied.

"You should have seen how long it took me to pull this together."

"It's the end result that matters, *amiga.*"

Before she knew it, Tiffany was the center of attention. Several people joined their group, and conversation about marital bliss took a backseat to discussion on the available bachelors in the room, courtesy of Norma Jean.

"We're here to have a good time, remember?" Tiffany pointed out. "Don't worry about me. I'm too busy for a serious relationship. My shop is the love of my life right now."

"Honey, you work too much. What you need is the love of a good man to keep you warm at night, not a laptop."

They all turned to see Norma Jean standing behind them.

A red tint spread across Tiffany's face. She tried to hide her embarrassment. "I'm fine…really."

Adrian wrapped an arm around his mother. "You heard her, Mom. Time for us to butt out."

"Mmm-hmm. That's what you and your buddies said over the last few years, and look what happened. I found perfect women for you—and the rest is history." Norma Jean beamed with pride. "Another love connection for the Love Broker."

Everyone laughed at Norma Jean's use of their nickname for her.

"If I remember correctly, I couldn't stand your son when I met him," Milán said sweetly.

"And then I turned on the charm, and you were a goner," Adrian boasted.

The whole group let out a collective groan.

Norma Jean turned to Tiffany. "What you need, dear, are my expert matchmaking skills. Don't worry, lovebird, I'll find your mate soon enough. You need to make time for some—"

"Jeannie," Milán said quickly. "Isn't it time for Adrian and my first dance?"

"You heard my blushing bride, Mom. *Tiempo de bailar!* Time to dance."

Norma Jean gasped. "Come on, you two," she said, ushering the couple away.

Tiffany mouthed a "thank you" to her best friend before she left to dance.

Tiffany was in a mood by the time she arrived home. She glanced across the hall to Milán's old apartment. She missed her friend. Now more than ever, Tiffany wished she were there to talk things over with while eating a pint of their favorite ice cream and watching a good movie. With a loud sigh, she locked the door behind her and headed straight for the bedroom.

After a shower, she slipped on a pair of pajama bottoms and a T-shirt before going to the kitchen to retrieve a spoon and a cup of ice cream. Returning, Tiffany plopped down on the bed. While she ate, she contemplated Norma Jean's words. Was she lonely? Was her job destined to be her only meaningful relationship?

Her store did take up a lot of time, but she loved it, and wanted her business to thrive. Still, she missed having a special man in her life to hang out with, share her thoughts with. *Having someone share your bed wouldn't be bad, either.*

Her phone vibrated. She set her cup on the nightstand and picked it up.

She was surprised to see a missed call from Ivan. She dialed voice mail, and Ivan's warm, deep voice filled her ear.

"Hello, Tiffany. This is Ivan Mangum. I have your quote ready. Call me, and we'll schedule a time to meet."

She listened to him recite his telephone number. Twice. She checked the time. It was almost eleven. She pondered if it was too late to call. Being ex-army, wasn't he used to late hours?

Tiffany dialed his number and waited. She prepared to leave a message, but was startled when Ivan picked on the second ring.

"Oh...hi. It's Tiffany. I hope I'm not disturbing you. I didn't know if it was too late to call."

"Of course not." There was surprise in his voice. "Are you available on Monday to go over my proposal?"

"Uh, sure."

"Great, how about three o'clock?"

"That's fine."

"Good. See you Monday."

She nodded as though he could see her.

"Good night, Tiffany. Have a great weekend."

Unable to stop herself, she grinned at his use of her name.

"Good night, Ivan, and you do the same."

Tiffany returned her phone to the nightstand and replayed the conversation in her head. His voice was so sexy. It resonated in her ear when he said her name. A tingle shot down her spine. Unable to help herself, Tiffany thought about seeing him again.

Being attracted to him would probably turn out to be a colossal waste of time, but for right now, in this moment, she allowed herself to revel in the excitement of how he made her feel. After turning out the light and pulling up the covers, she closed her eyes, and Ivan instantly appeared—just as sexy and compelling as he was in person.

Her stomach quivered in reaction as though he were standing right there.

For tonight, the image of Ivan Mangum would have to do.

Chapter 4

The weekend flew by for Tiffany. On Monday, at three o'clock on the dot, Ivan walked through the door.

"Welcome back," she said.

"Thanks. I spotted a coffee shop down the street. I thought we could go there and talk."

"That's fine. I'll get my purse."

Tiffany went into the back room and retrieved her purse from a cabinet. She used a small mirror to freshen her makeup.

It's not a date, she scolded herself while applying lipstick. Tiffany returned to where Ivan was waiting. He held the door for her as they stepped outside into the afternoon sun.

"So how long have you been in the area?" he asked conversationally.

"A few years. I'm originally from Baltimore. I'm an only child, and thought that it was time to change scenery. I came here for a job and never left."

"Are you close with your parents?"

"For the most part. I miss having them nearby, but they visit when they can. Separately, of course. Together would be a definite nightmare, since they're divorced.

"And since my business started, I haven't really had the chance to get there as often as I'd like."

"What do your parents do?"

"My father is a principal at a high school, and my mother works in human resources at a global investment firm downtown." She turned to him. "What about you?"

"I was born here. My father was a colonel in the army, and my mother was a professor in the classics department at a local university. We traveled a lot, either for my mother's book research or when my father got new orders. In retrospect, my father played a large part in my decision to join the army and go to Officer Candidate School after college."

"That must've been fun."

"Loads." He laughed. "I've been out for a while and started my company two years ago. I've been pretty busy ever since."

"Well, on behalf of civilians everywhere, I want to thank you for protecting our freedom and liberties," she said.

A wide smile etched his face. "Thanks. It was my honor to serve my country."

He held the door to the coffee shop open. They placed their order, and Ivan insisted on paying.

Tiffany found a table, and he came over with their drinks.

She inhaled the aromatic smell of her chai latte. "You don't strike me as the tea type."

He glanced down at his green tea. A lopsided grin etched his face. "I only drink coffee when I'm on assignments."

"So you install security systems for a living?"

"No. I installed one a year ago for my grandmother's assisted-living facility and picked up a few more locations by word of mouth. I've done a few businesses in Chicago. One being the community center where Ms. Jeannie teaches classes. I've taught a few senior security classes there."

"You're big on security."

He laughed. "You could say that. My company, Mangum and Associates, specializes in personal protection for dignitaries, business executives and notables. We take long and short-term assignments."

"Wow, so you're like high-end bodyguards. Have you ever protected anyone famous?"

"A few," he admitted.

"Seeing all those new places must be exciting for you."

"Not all glitz and glamour, I assure you. It's plenty of long hours, even longer reports and not much of a social life. In fact, I live a pretty monklike existence."

"I'm familiar with that," she said drily. "Not the danger and intrigue, but the long hours, minuscule social life and loads of paperwork. So why the business of protection?"

Ivan shrugged. "It seemed a natural extension of my skill set, plus I enjoy it."

"I'm sure the world is a much safer place because of it," she said sincerely.

Ivan glanced up. Their gazes connected across the table.

Clearing his throat, he opened his laptop. "I suppose we should get started."

For the next thirty-five minutes, Ivan laid out his plan for Tiffany's store. He took into account everything she asked for, plus a few *Mission: Impossible*–type features that she didn't. When Tiffany started to protest, he cut her off.

"It wasn't as expensive as you think." He slid his laptop around to face her. "See?"

Tiffany scanned over the screen. She blinked a few times. "Wow, this is actually…affordable."

"I get discounts on the merchandise, and my fee is reasonable."

"Ivan, this seems like almost a pass-through on costs."

"I'm not doing this to become wealthy, Tiffany. This is more of a hobby for me. The work I do at Mangum is high stress, keeps me busy and affords a great living. The services I provide to the community allow me to give back."

She looked skeptical.

"It's true." He chuckled. "Now stop worrying, and tell me when you'd like to get started. It won't take more than an evening or two to get it done. We work at night so there's no interruption to you or your customers."

"We?"

"I'll be getting my brother, Cole, to help out," he explained. "It will go much faster that way."

"You have a brother? I don't know why, but I assumed you were an only child."

"Cole is my younger brother. It's just the two of us. I think we exhausted our parents, so they quit while they were ahead," he joked.

"My parents weren't able to have more children, so I was it. Normally, I don't miss having a sibling, but there are times when it would be nice to have more family—or at least a buffer every now and then."

Ivan glanced over with a quizzical expression.

"They argued a lot toward the end. It was intense at times," she explained.

That caused Ivan to frown. "I bet that was hard on you."

She shrugged. "Kids are resilient. I learned to cope." Tiffany played with her cup. "You know, I cried with relief when they told me they were getting divorced."

"I'm sorry to hear that."

"I wasn't. Besides, I got another bedroom to call my own, so it all worked out. But enough about me. What about you?"

"My parents are still married and in love. Which only makes them more interested in what my brother and I are up to," he said, trying to interject some levity.

"Sounds like they'd get along quite well with Ms. Jeannie," Tiffany joked.

Ivan observed various emotions cross Tiffany's face. She wasn't as unaffected by her family's problems as she tried to portray. There was real pain in her expression and body language. Before he knew it, he reached across the table and covered her hand with his. He squeezed it reassuringly, giving her some of his strength. A shocked expression crossed her face momentarily, but then she relaxed.

"I'll bet your rooms were every teenage girl's dream." He watched a few tears glisten in her eyes before she blinked them away.

She laughed. "Maybe not, but I thought they were pretty cool."

He released her hand. To give her a chance to compose herself, Ivan relayed some tales of his childhood. The sparkle in her eyes slowly returned, and she even chimed in with some funny stories of her own. Reluctantly, their discussion returned to work, and they were able to finalize the plans and payment arrangements. When they were done, Ivan escorted Tiffany back to her store. He held the door open for her, but stopped just inside.

"Thanks for this afternoon. And thank you for the wonderful security system, Ivan."

He chuckled. "That's the first time someone's thanked me in advance."

"That's because I know I'll love it."

"Then you're welcome…in advance." He smiled broadly. "Cole and I will see you on Wednesday."

"Great, and thanks again."

Ivan took her hand in his again and squeezed. "Anytime."

Moments later, Ivan was getting into his SUV. Their afternoon together had been illuminating. He learned that Tiffany held a lot inside, and that her emotions ran deep. He was surprised that sharing a few of her childhood memories had caused her composure to slip. Seeing her distressed like that had stirred something inside him. He barely knew her, and yet wanted nothing more than to protect her from the sadness lurking behind her eyes.

Then he recalled his vow on remaining strictly professional. Cole would have a field day when he found out Ivan's latest predicament. With a wry smile, he started his truck and pulled off.

Inside the store, Tiffany's sales associate, Celeste, came over to her. "Aside from having lunch with a bona fide hunk, what's got you in such a good mood?"

"It wasn't lunch," Tiffany corrected. "It was a business meeting. I'm getting a new security system for the store. It's long overdue."

The younger woman tilted her head to the side. "Are you sure it's not the man installing it that's got you so happy?"

"Don't be silly." Tiffany tried to sound stern, but failed miserably. She couldn't help the smile that spread across her face. "He's simply doing a favor for a mutual friend. Nothing more."

"Sure he is."

In truth, Tiffany hardly believed her own words, either. The second his hand touched hers at the café, a spark had flickered inside. The prospect of seeing him again was exciting, but grinning from ear to ear would blow her cover. She started to tell herself that he was a regular guy, but stopped. Not for one second was Ivan Mangum a regular anything.

Tiffany decided to call Milán to get a second opinion. The moment she answered, Tiffany whispered into the receiver, "I've got a dilemma."

"What's his name?"

Tiffany hesitated. She was about to step off a precipice, and when she did, there was no going back. With a deep breath, she said, "It's…Ivan Mangum."

"You mean the—"

"Yes."

"With the—"

"Yes," she interjected again. "But you can't tell Jeannie, Milán."

"Why not?"

"Are you kidding? If she hears that I find Ivan as delectable as a Krispy Kreme doughnut, she'll be all over me like cling wrap to stake my claim on him."

"And what's wrong with that? You should snap him up before someone else notices that he's single, attractive and a good guy."

"Yeah about that—don't you find it odd that he's even available?" Tiffany countered. "Maybe he's got seven kids in four different cities, or he's commitment-shy?"

"Tiff, has it ever occurred to you that he could be single for the same reasons you are? Need I remind you of Adrian and me?"

"No," she said quickly. "I get it. Maybe nothing's wrong with him, and he's single for no good reason…"

"It's possible he hasn't found the right person—just like you."

Tiffany sighed. "Okay, I'll give him the benefit of the doubt."

"I'm glad. And you will be, too."

"We'll see."

"So how long do you think it'll take Norma Jean to figure out you like Ivan?"

"There's no way I'm telling her anytime soon."

"Trust me, if she gets a whiff of attraction, she'll ply you with questions until you crack and spill the beans—I've been there. And if she sees you and Ivan together…"

With a gasp, Tiffany said, "That can't happen, Milán, I mean it. Under no circumstances is Norma Jean to find out that I think of Ivan as anything but the guy who's installing my security system."

"It's not me you have to worry about, *chica,*" Milán said.

She was right. Adrian's mother had X-ray vision when it came to seeing what people didn't want revealed, and her inconvenient habit of not being able to say Ivan's name without smiling would be as noticeable as a flare shot into the sky. "Let's face it, I'm screwed."

"Don't say that," Milán admonished. "You'll be fine. Besides, Norma Jean won't be there Wednesday."

"True," Tiffany said with relief. "I don't know what the heck's wrong with me. Normally, I'm unflappable."

"Totally unflappable." Her friend snickered.

"I can do this. The next time he walks through that door, I'll be cool and strictly professional. Mark my words, Operation Dry Ice is in effect," Tiffany said, with feeling.

Now if she could only get her heart on board with the plan.

Chapter 5

The shrill ring of Ivan's cell phone woke him up. Instantly alert, he retrieved it from his nightstand. "Mangum."

"I'm sorry to bother you at home, sir," his assistant, Curtis, said in a worried voice. "I'm afraid we have a situation. One that demands your immediate attention."

"Sure, Curtis, what's up?"

"There was an incident in Vancouver. Our client is fine," his assistant assured him, "but Daniels was busted up pretty bad. I've sent another member of the team to take over, but…the client is insisting that you come personally."

Ivan swore under his breath. "Understood. Make the arrangements. We'll leave as soon as the plane's ready. I want a briefing on the situation by the time wheels are up."

"Yes, sir."

He hung up and strode to his closet to start packing. *Damn.* He'd tell Cole his plans on the way out. Right now, Ivan needed to gather all the facts about the mishap to do damage control. At Mangum, an unhappy client was completely unacceptable.

* * *

On Wednesday, Tiffany closed up the shop early to accommodate Ivan and his brother. She set out snacks and drinks on the table in the storage room. She was working on inventory orders when a man walked through the door.

She knew immediately that he was Ivan's brother. The resemblance was strong, but Ivan was broader in build, taller, and his eyes were more golden. She went to greet him. "You must be Cole." She smiled.

He shook her hand. "I am. How are you, Miss Gentry?"

"I'm well, and call me Tiffany. Thanks for coming." She looked behind him to see another man following. They made introductions. "Good to meet you, John." Tiffany couldn't help but ask, "Is Ivan on his way?"

Cole shook his head. "He's been unavoidably detained. He asked me to apologize, and to let you know he'll arrive as soon as he can."

"Oh. No problem. I'll show you around."

Tiffany was disappointed, but tried to hide it. A short time later, Milán and Norma Jean came through the door.

When she saw them, she had to stifle a groan. "What a nice surprise," Tiffany said pointedly.

"Isn't it? Jeannie thought you'd like to join us for dinner," Milán replied brightly.

"Yeah, and I wanted to see how Ivan was working out," Norma Jean added.

Tiffany schooled her features. She didn't need Norma Jean's radar going off. "Oh, well, Colonel Mangum isn't here, but should be soon. Dinner sounds great. I'll go get my purse." She sped off.

"Hello, Cole," Norma Jean said when she spotted him. She walked over and hugged him. "Deciding to give the ladies a break this evening?"

"Now why would I do that, Ms. Jeannie?" Cole grinned. "Besides, it's early yet."

"Scoundrel," she replied in mock disapproval. "Where's that brother of yours? He'd better not be loafing around. I talked him up to Tiffany, so my reputation is on the line."

"Don't worry, it's still intact," Ivan called from the doorway.

Tiffany's pulse quickened. He wore army fatigues, and looked more delectable than usual.

He went straight to Tiffany. "I'm sorry I'm late. I had an emergency crop up at work."

It was tough concentrating on the words with his face inches away. His close proximity wreaked havoc on her senses.

"No problem," she assured him. "The guys are moving right along."

"Glad to hear it." He turned to the other women. "How are you ladies?"

"Fine," Norma Jean replied. "We're going to dinner. Care to join us?"

"No, ma'am. We've got work to do." He and Cole exchanged glances. His brother nodded. "We'll be finished by the time you return."

"Can I bring you something back?" Tiffany offered.

"We're good, thanks," Cole chimed in.

Norma Jean swung into action. "You heard the man. Let's get a move on. I'm hungry, and the lines aren't getting any shorter."

The moment they left, Ivan turned to his brother.

"How are we really doing?"

Cole rolled his eyes. "Ivan, it's not rocket science. I've got this."

"Uh-huh."

He flooded Cole with a barrage of questions. With a loud sigh, Cole brought him up to speed. Walking around, Ivan began spot-checking his brother's work.

"Top-notch," he confirmed after a full inspection.

"Thank you, Colonel Mangum," Cole replied with a salute before giving his brother an "I told you so" look. Ivan was about to walk away when Cole said, "She's fine, by the way."

"Cole," Ivan ground out.

"I'm just saying, she's a cute little thing. Kind of short for you, isn't she? But then again, you can make up the difference when you're horizontal—"

A small box sailed past Cole's head. He reached out and caught it. He flashed a huge grin at his brother. "You'll have to do better than that."

"The next time it'll be my fist," Ivan promised.

Outside, Tiffany realized she'd forgotten her cell phone in the store. She promised Norma Jean and Milán she'd be right back, then hurried into the boutique and over to the counter. As she grabbed her phone, she overheard Cole and Ivan talking in the storage room.

"She was the reason you were late?"

Tiffany stopped in her tracks. She definitely did not want to be caught eavesdropping, and yet she could not bring herself to move.

"No," Ivan answered. "I was dealing with that mess Daniels created in Canada."

"So all is well," Cole said.

"Not for Daniels. He had two drinks while on duty. Company policy is no drinking while on the clock—no exceptions. He's on probation."

"Don't you think you're being a bit hard on him?"

"Hell, no. He's lucky I didn't fire him. In our line of work, there can be no distractions, Cole. Situations can turn into life-or-death scenarios in an instant, and my employees have to be prepared—for anything. I can't risk them being impaired. Daniels was dead wrong, and there are consequences."

"So where does Debra fit into the scenario?"

Unable to help herself, Tiffany inched closer.

"She contacted the office, and they patched her through."

"Can't you see what she's up to? You're her ace in the hole—you've always been."

"I made a promise, and if Debra needs me, I'll be there. End of story."

That was her cue. Tiffany backed up the way she'd come, almost knocking over a display. Steadying it, Tiffany made a stealthy retreat. Her hand was on the doorknob when Ivan's voice stopped her.

"Hey. I didn't know you'd come back."

Tiffany stopped and cursed her bad timing. She plastered a smile on her face and turned around. "Yeah, I forgot my cell phone." She held it up. "I gotta run, though. Norma Jean's going to have a cow if I take any longer."

"Sure. I'll be by in the morning to go over everything. How's nine?"

"Great. See you then." She made a beeline outside, closing the door behind her.

You've got half a block to make it look like nothing's wrong.

"What could be wrong?" she said aloud. "I have no claims on him. We're not dating. I thought he was cute, right? Nothing more. If he wants to pledge his undying love to Debra, he can go right ahead."

With a superhuman effort, she got into the car and cheerfully said, "I got it."

"Wonderful," Norma Jean replied. "So where are we going to eat?"

"How about Rajun Cajun?" Tiffany said. "I could use a little something spicy."

Norma Jean didn't miss a beat. "Well, if you'd let me

fix you up like I've been wanting to, you'd have all the spice you need."

Milán laughed. "You knew she wasn't gonna leave that one alone."

Tiffany muttered something in agreement, and then turned her head to gaze out the window.

He's taken. Crap.

An eclectic blend of New Orleans and New Delhi cuisines, the Rajun Cajun restaurant in Hyde Park was a favorite for soul food and traditional Indian dishes. After studying the menu, they placed their orders. While waiting, Tiffany recalled Ivan's conversation with Cole. Hearing them discuss Ivan's girlfriend had made her stomach clench. Granted, she didn't know him that well, and had no claim on his affections, but it was still disheartening.

"So, Tiffany, I was thinking that this Saturday would be perfect for a date, don't you agree?"

"Sure," she said absentmindedly. "I'll be there."

"Great."

When their orders were ready, Norma Jean invited them over to her house, but Tiffany wasn't up for company.

"I'll pass if you don't mind. It's been a long day, and I'm beat."

Milán dropped her back at the store to pick up her car.

"Thanks, and sorry I'm bailing on you."

"Honey, it happens," Norma Jean responded. "We'll touch base later about Saturday. I'm so excited."

Tiffany waved goodbye, and was about to get into her car when she looked at her boutique. Ivan and his crew were gone. It was dark inside, except for the muted shades of pink emanating from a miniature poodle night-light at the back of the store. It was there less for security, and more because she thought it was cute and wanted something whimsical to remind her to smile. She could use that right about now.

Tiffany got into her car and headed home. While she was watching TV, Milán called.

"Hey, Lani, what's up?"

"That's what I'd like to know. Why'd you agree to go out on a blind date after telling me four times that you weren't taking Jeannie up on her offer to fix you up?"

"Huh? I never said I'd go out with anyone."

"Oh, you sure did," her friend countered. "Tonight at Rajun Cajun. You said you'd go out with Gardiniér this Saturday."

"What?" Tiffany exclaimed. "Who's Gardiniér? I didn't know that's what I was agreeing to. I thought she'd asked me about…well, I don't know what, but certainly not a date. Why didn't you stop me?"

"Me? How was I to know you hadn't changed your mind?"

Tiffany leaned back on the couch. "Is that his first or last name?"

"Uh, I think it's his first."

"That's his real name? This is a disaster."

"Don't I know it," Milán agreed. "Tell her you had no idea what she asked you. What had you so spaced out, anyway?"

"Ivan and his girlfriend, Debra," Tiffany blurted out before she could stop herself.

"He has a girlfriend? How did the Love Broker miss that?"

"It's not important," Tiffany hedged.

"Apparently it is if you're so out of sorts. Are you sure?"

"Yes. I overheard him this evening when I went back to get my phone. Her name is Debra, and apparently she needs him desperately," Tiffany stressed, and then realized she sounded catty.

"Well, that sucks. I'm sorry, Tiff."

"Me, too. Enough about Ivan Mangum. Let's forget it, and I'm not taking Norma Jean up on her offer."

Milán choked on whatever she was drinking. "You aren't? How are you getting out of it?"

"I don't know, but I'll think of something."

"Good, then you can come over Saturday for movie night with me and Adrian."

"Thanks for the invite, but I think I'll pass. You guys have fun. I've got to call Jeannie now and get it over with."

"Good luck."

"Thanks." She hung up, then dialed Norma Jean. She hoped to get voice mail, but no such luck.

"Hi, Ms. Jeannie. How are you?"

"Just fine, honey. Trying to keep my husband from cheating in Scrabble. I've got to challenge every word he puts down. Get the dictionary, Cliff," Norma Jean said distractedly. "No, moarting is not a word."

"Um, the reason I called is that I…I can't make the date this Saturday," Tiffany said quickly. "I wasn't paying attention when you mentioned it, and I've got plans."

"Oh. Poor Gardiniér. He'll be disappointed."

"I'm sorry, Ms. Jeannie. Thanks again for understanding," Tiffany said.

"Oh, sure dear. I'll call him just as soon as Cliff and I finish our game, which won't be long. Why I let him talk me into this bootleg game is anybody's guess. Good night, honey, I'll talk to you later."

She hung up. "Well, that's one Gardiniér who won't be landscaping my rosebush."

Chapter 6

"You know, when I came to celebrate, this wasn't what I had in mind." Ivan handed his grandmother her ice cream, and then parked his SUV alongside the ice-cream parlor.

"Hey, I'm sick of sitting around watching television all day," Cecile Mangum replied. "It's my birthday. I wanted a change of scenery, and you're the only one of us with a driver's license. I really appreciate you taking me to my favorite ice-cream parlor, honey. Of course, if you prefer that I take the wheel I…"

"Oh, no, you don't, Speed Racer. I can manage."

Ivan's grandmother snorted. "I go through one little red light, and the whole community is up in arms."

"GiGi, you almost caused a four-car pileup behind you. Not to mention the couple on the park bench."

"Hey, they moved, didn't they?"

"Luckily for you, they were still able to," Ivan pointed out. "Not everyone that old is that limber."

"Presumably that's why you're here. I do appreciate the visit," she replied.

Ivan reached over and squeezed her heavily veined hand. "It's my pleasure."

"I love my gift. How'd you know I like owls?"

"I didn't." His thoughts drifted to Tiffany. "I had some help trying to find something nearly as wise as you."

"Scoundrel." She chuckled. "And where's that other rascal?"

"Cole had to work late. He'll see you tomorrow."

"Work indeed." She took a spoonful of her chocolate sundae. "My grandson is probably out chasing skirts. Mangum men have always been charmers. You know, when your granddaddy was alive, he could charm me right out of my—"

Ivan quickly put up a hand to stop her. He took a healthy sip of his milk shake.

"Saints preserve me. You aren't sitting next to the Virgin Mary, you know. It ain't over till it's over."

Ivan looked decidedly uncomfortable. "Next subject, please?"

"Fine. If you don't want to talk about my love life, how about yours?"

"There's nothing to tell, GiGi. I'm not seeing anyone."

"Hmm…I hear a restless note in your voice, honey. You need to make time for romance, and don't give me that gibberish about work."

"It's not gibberish. I'm proud of what I do."

"Yes, but can work get you a date?"

"I have a policy about not fraternizing with my employees…in that capacity."

"Bah. Do you have a policy for everything? How boring is that? Ivan, work doesn't keep you warm at night, or fill you with a burning desire to—"

"I get it," he interrupted again.

"My body is old, sweetheart, not the mind. You need to find a woman who can make you happy…make your soul smile. That's the kind of connection I had with your grandfather. It's rare enough to find without you purpose-fully overlooking it."

That made Ivan smile. He leaned over and kissed his grandmother's cheek. "Who says I've overlooked it? What makes you think I'd bring every girl I date here?"

Cecile did a double take. "Every? Hell, how about any?"

Ivan stayed another few minutes, sparring with his grandmother before escorting her back to the assisted-living facility. On the drive home, he pondered her words. Some of her advice was spot-on. Ivan was stuck in a rut, and he needed to shake things up.

When it came to relationships, the challenge had been maintaining them. When he loved, he was all in. There was no in-between. Debra was the last woman he'd given his heart to, and she had handed it back with artillery shells in it. It hadn't been loaned out since. There'd been women, but it was strictly physical, or as his grandmother put it, to get his ice-cream cone dipped once in a while. She was incor-rigible. Cecile Mangum was a virtuoso at human nature, and seeing someone's true colors. If Ivan could've done that half as well, he'd have saved himself a lot of heartache.

Debra's deception had cut deep, but it was history. Ivan had survived. Now a new woman had caught his eye and breathed life back into him. She was exciting and beautiful.

Yes, definitely time to move on.

Tiffany spotted Ivan walk in. "Damn, you're good! I love it," she said excitedly.

"That's good to hear," he replied.

The Petite Boutique was not officially open, so they were alone.

"No, really. I love hearing the chime when the door

opens. To know I've got 24/7 monitoring gives me a sense of security, and the surveillance feature…wow," she exclaimed. "That I can be home and use my laptop to see the inside of my store blows my mind."

It was hard not to get caught up in her excitement. Her eyes sparkled with it. Ivan was unable to keep from grinning, either. "Then I've done my job. I promised you *Mission: Impossible,* but on a budget," he teased.

Ivan showed Tiffany more features and set up her surveillance program on her laptop. He helped her through the tutorial, as well as pointed out additional upgrades she could get later.

"Thank you for doing all this for me, Ivan."

"It's been my pleasure, Tiffany."

Her associate, Celeste, walked through the door. When it chimed, the two shared a smile.

She walked him out. "So what's next for you?"

"Jeannie asked me to conduct another senior safety class."

"That sounds like fun."

Suddenly, Ivan's expression turned mischievous. "Great. I need an assistant."

She stopped smiling. "Me? Huh? I… No, I couldn't. I'd be terrible at it."

"I doubt it. You said you'd taken self-defense classes before."

"Yeah, but that was some time ago."

"So you're saying you can't do it?"

There was a hint of challenge in his voice that ruffled Tiffany's competitive side. She nodded before her cautious side could catch up. "I'll do it. When is it?"

"Tonight. The name of the class will be on the door. If there's a change, I'll call you."

"I don't know, Ivan, I—"

Without warning, he held a finger up to her lips to silence her. She stilled.

"Tiffany?"

"Hmm?" She mumbled around his hand.

"Say yes."

He moved his finger from her lips, but remained in close proximity.

"Yes," she heard herself whisper.

The air crackled with tension. Unable to help herself, she gravitated toward him. They stood there for infinite moments staring at each other until a horn broke the spell.

Ivan backed up. "I'll see you tonight at five. I'll text you the address. Traffic may be rough, so give yourself extra time to get there. Bye, Tiffany."

Without another word, Ivan was gone, leaving her standing on the sidewalk in front of her store with a baffled expression on her face. She raised a hand up to her mouth. His hold over her in that moment was complete and all-consuming.

When she regained her wits, Tiffany was mortified. The worst realization was that she had *wanted* a kiss to happen, more than she wanted to take her next breath.

Tiffany gazed after him until his Range Rover was out of sight. *Ivan's lips and everything else on him are off-limits.* She vowed to repeat the sentence like a litany for the rest of the day in hopes of remembering that he was already taken, and to stop her heart, mind and soul from pining for a man she could never have.

Hours later, Tiffany arrived home worn-out, and no closer to not thinking about Ivan Mangum than before. After showering and putting on workout clothes, she surveyed herself in the mirror. Tiffany was nervous. Attending an exercise class was one thing, but being up there with the instructor was completely different. Especially when the instructor was Ivan.

"You can do this," she said to her reflection.

Ivan had thrown down a challenge, and she planned to show him she could deliver. Their encounter outside of her store came to mind. Feeling his finger on her lips was flat-out shocking…and sensuous! Thank goodness he'd left before she'd voiced the desire to kiss him. She checked the clock, then grabbed her gym bag and headed out the door.

The community center was located in Washington Park on the South Side of Chicago. Tiffany parked and strolled into the building. She had a few minutes to spare, so she unpacked a yoga mat and warmed up. She was on her last rep of stretches when Ivan walked in.

"Hey."

"Hey," she responded. Tiffany rolled up her mat. "I was warming up."

"Good. Our class should start in a few minutes."

Ivan dropped his bag in a corner and strode over. "I'm glad you made it."

"Of course—especially since you practically made me. Something you picked up in the military, huh, Yoda?"

He burst out laughing. "Well, apparently it worked. You're here, and I'm grateful," he said quietly.

Tiffany tried not to fall under his spell a second time. It was hard when he was looking at her with that same intense look as earlier. *When you almost kissed him.*

She tried to dismiss it, but it was hard to let go. The fact that he was wearing more physique-enhancing active wear didn't help.

"So what's on the agenda?" she asked, trying to ignore his effect on her.

"I'd like to cover some basic moves our group can learn to ward off would-be attackers. If they're approached by someone bent on doing them harm, they can't outrun their assailant. They'll need to stand their ground. That won't be expected by most purse snatchers. They'll be expecting the flight-or-fight mechanism to kick in and will use it to their advantage to overpower the elderly person and take what they want."

"Or worse, do them bodily harm."

"Exactly. I'll touch on situational awareness, too. Knowing what's going on around them can decrease the chances of being approached by someone waiting to strike. We'll cover the basics, but most importantly, we're going to have some fun and get some exercise."

"You got it, Coach Mangum," Tiffany said. "I'm ready."

Ivan's class lasted an hour. He started with an informational session about himself and his background. Tiffany learned that he'd traveled many places, had trained with military personnel in over six countries, was fluent in several languages, an expert marksman, and studied mixed martial arts for the past few years.

In addition to being a lethal weapon, he was all business when it came to teaching the elderly how to protect themselves. She assisted him by demonstrating how to render an attacker senseless with a few well-placed Cane-Fu moves using their canes as a weapon.

Next, Ivan showed them palms to the nose, kicks to the groin, gouges to the eye and punches to the trachea. Ivan used Tiffany as the aggressor to show the class how to protect against a side-arm grab and a two-handed collar grab. Afterward, he checked people's posture to ensure they were doing the moves effectively and without injury.

The hour flew by for Tiffany. She was actually disappointed when it came to an end. Quite a few people praised her efforts.

"I hope you'll be coming back, little lady," one man said.

"I'll be here whenever Coach Mangum needs me," she promised.

When the last of the students had left, Ivan came up to her.

"I thought that went well."

"Well is an understatement," she said. "Ivan, what you did for the class was inspiring. You could see their self-confidence growing as they learned and practiced each move. It's a great feeling to be able to help someone overcome their fears and to give them the knowledge they need to allow them to feel empowered, to know that they have it within themselves to fight back if the situation arises."

"Exactly," he said eagerly. "The most important thing is getting the time needed to get away safely, or to render the bad guy incapacitated so they can get help."

"You did a wonderful thing."

He grinned down at her. "We did a wonderful thing. You were great."

Tiffany couldn't help the warmth that crept up her cheeks. "It was easy. You're good at this. People can't help but feel safer when you're around."

"Speaking of safe, how's the security system working for you?"

"It's been great, and I feel much safer now. Taking your class helped, too. I've learned a lot of ways to protect myself. Especially escaping a bear-hug hold."

"Remember, the key to the bear-hug breakaway is to hook your foot around your attacker's leg. Then both your hands go immediately to his, and then grab a finger or thumb and pull away from the body to break the hold."

Before Tiffany could reply, Ivan dipped behind her and grabbed her waist. She immediately hooked one leg around his, and then planted her other foot. Tiffany put her hands on his arms, pushed down and then grabbed his thumb. She pushed it back.

"Good, now follow up with kicks to the groin and solar plexus, or elbows to the neck and face."

They practiced a few times. Ivan was a big man, and though he did not use his full weight while going through the motions, Tiffany was still winded.

He nodded with approval. "Much better, but remember—" he grabbed her suddenly and spun her away from him so that her back was flush against his front "—quick blows, and then get out of there." His breath caressed her ear in an intimate whisper. "And never, ever let your guard down."

He turned her again so that they were facing each other, but he did not release her. Her arms came up to his shoulders to steady herself. Tiffany was breathing heavily from the exertion—or was it the close proximity to Ivan? She honestly didn't know.

"Thank you for showing me that technique. You must be good at a lot of these."

He chuckled. "I've had a great deal of practice over the years."

Tiffany's eyes met his. A warm heat spread from the lower half of her body upward. Her voice was barely above a whisper when she said, "I'll bet."

His eyes darkened instantly. Tiffany was too caught up in the sudden predatory gleam in his eye to move. Mortified at her own words, she blushed. "What I meant was…"

"You didn't mean to give me a compliment?" he asked.

"No, I was…just not like *that*."

Ivan lowered his arms, and she was free. Tiffany felt the rush of space between them. It was hard not to protest at the loss of warmth from his embrace.

"How about I walk you out?"

"Sure."

He escorted her to her car and made sure she was inside and settled. He sat back on his haunches so they were eye level.

"Thanks again for coming."

"My pleasure."

"Good night, Tiffany. Ring me one when you get home so that I know you're safe."

She looked surprised. "Oh, sure."

He stood up, tapped her door, and then moved back. Tiffany waved and drove away.

She decided to take the long way home to give herself some time to process what had happened after their exercise class. Out of the blue, their light, jovial manner had changed to something thick, tangible and most definitely sexual.

Recalling their conversation sent tingles throughout her body. She had never been that suggestive before, but being alone with Ivan after such a hands-on type of class made the nerve endings in her body go supercharged. She could feel an undercurrent. His amber eyes reminded her of a tiger's, making her wonder if there were a few seconds before being devoured that the jungle cat's prey stood mesmerized by the sheer hypnotic effect of its golden gaze.

The feeling was similar to observing one of her favorite paintings. The longer she stared at it, the more she wanted to stare.

When she was wrapped in Ivan's ironclad embrace, the only thing on her mind was that she wanted him to kiss her. Not the quick peck on the lips, but the most thorough, deep, erotic kiss she'd ever had in her life.

As Ivan drove home, he thought about his evening. He had enjoyed teaching the seniors' class—and spending time with Tiffany.

Who are you kidding? It's the most fun you've had in a while.

He thought about the gleam in Tiffany's eyes when she took him down for the first time. There was such a sense of accomplishment and confidence in her expression that he had to chuckle. Before she got back to business, she took a victory lap around the class that reminded him of Sylvester Stallone jumping up and down in triumph in the movie *Rocky.* She was something else.

He also recounted their playful banter and how, seconds later, it took everything in him not to grab her and claim her sexy mouth for a searing kiss. His body reacted instantly to the memory of how good she looked. Suddenly uncomfortable at the tightness below his waist, Ivan shifted a few times in his seat.

His cell phone rang. Thankful for the distraction, Ivan answered. "Hey, Cole. What's up?"

"You done with class?"

"Yeah, why?"

"How about dinner at Giordano's?"

"Sure. I'll get us a table."

Ivan arrived and ordered a beer. As he sipped it, he thought about his social life. GiGi was right. It was pretty boring. It was all work and family obligations. Not that he would ever shirk one of his responsibilities. Ivan was overzealous when it came to doing what was expected of him. The army had amplified that mantra. Still, there was more out there, and it was passing him by.

His thoughts strayed to Debra. Pain and remorse wrapped themselves around his heart like a vise grip.

"You're scaring potential dates off," Cole greeted him, sitting down.

Ivan pushed away the melancholy. "I'll do my best."

Since they already knew the menu, they ordered a deep-dish pizza with everything on it.

"So how was class?" Cole asked after their server left.

"Good. Tiffany was a fantastic assistant," he said proudly. "You should've seen her."

"Tiffany helped teach your class? As in, 'she's my client,' Tiffany?"

"Yes."

"What happened to that whole rule thing?"

"Technically, she's not my client anymore," Ivan pointed out.

"Great. Does that mean you're going to ask her out?"

Ivan was silent.

"Don't even try to convince me that you don't want to. You should've seen your face when you described your evening. I thought you were going to need a towel to wipe the drool."

Ivan grinned and took another sip of beer. "Shut up."

"Dude, tell me I'm wrong," Cole countered. "I don't know why you're trying to act like you aren't attracted to her."

"That's not what I'm doing. In fact—"

Cole sat back in his chair. "Then what are you doing, Ivan?" He interrupted. "I've seen her. The woman is seriously working the hotness factor. Plus, she's warm, funny and for whatever reason likes you. You scowl all the time, have no sense of humor and no love life. Why all that drives women out of their panties, I'll never know."

Ivan glanced over at his brother. "Wait…how do you know she likes me?"

Cole shook his head. "You're pathetic."

"What?"

"How is it you can hear a grenade pin being pulled from twenty clicks away, you're a weapon unto yourself, an expert strategist, and can speak not one, but several languages in addition to English, but something as rudimentary as a woman who can't keep her eyes off you goes poof…right over your head?"

"Okay, it's not twenty clicks, and you have two seconds to answer the question," Ivan warned.

Cole took a pull on the beer he had been given. "In that whole list of stuff, that's all you got out of it?"

Ivan stared at him.

Cole shook his head. "It's *how* she looks at you when she thinks nobody is looking, Ivan. She hangs on your every word, and the most telling sign was when you arrived late the other night and she thought you weren't coming. She looked like someone had kicked her puppy."

Ivan took a breath, then said, "Earlier this afternoon, we almost kissed."

Cole leaned back in his chair with a shocked but satisfied grin. "Tell me everything."

Ivan filled his brother in on his day and the connection he felt with Tiffany. Cole listened intently. When Ivan was finished, Cole said, "So what's with the long face?"

"It's...complicated."

"What is? Call her up, take her on a proper date and get this thing going. What am I missing?"

Ivan frowned. "Debra."

Cole let out an expletive. "I told you to take care of that situation, but you didn't listen. Now you have to clear the air with Tiffany, and you know how that's going to go."

"I know," Ivan replied. "I'm not sure she's going to understand."

"To be honest, big brother, I don't understand why she's still in your life. Cut her loose, and be done with it."

"Debra and I were over a long time ago. She made her choice, and I respected it. I didn't like it, but I didn't have much of a choice, did I? She picked Brian to spend her life with, and I've been dealing with that decision ever since."

"But you haven't let go."

Ivan's expression darkened. "You know I don't have feelings for her anymore."

"What I know, big brother, is that you're in a complicated mess because you're too damn noble to extricate yourself from it. While I can, though I don't understand it, appreciate your dedication to friends, promises and what you consider your obligations, I'm at a loss to understand how you're going to get Tiffany to understand this mess you're in—or to be okay with it."

Ivan swirled the beer around in his mug. "I know."

Cole held up his beer in a toast. "Here's to things working out the way you want."

Ivan raised his mug, and then downed his beer. "It will. Failure's not an option."

Chapter 7

How do you celebrate having avoided another bad romance? With a darn good dinner. Tiffany took a sip of wine and put her feet up on the coffee table. First, a sumptuous meal, and then a movie. She raised her glass and toasted herself. "Works for me."

When the phone rang, she leaned over and answered it.

"Hello?"

"Hey, Tiffany...were you busy?"

She bolted upright. "Hi, Ivan. No, not really. What's up?"

"Well, I just got home from doing an install. I know it's short notice, but would you like to grab a bite to eat?"

Her eyes grew wide. "I—I, um..."

"I get it, now's not the best time—"

"No, it's not that," she said quickly.

She glanced toward the kitchen. "But what if you come here? I'm sort of in the middle of cooking dinner. You're welcome to join me. I have plenty."

"Are you sure it's not an inconvenience? We can make it another time if you'd prefer."

"It's no imposition, Ivan. Can you head over now? Dinner's almost ready."

"Sure. Text me your address."

"Okay."

"Great, I'll see you shortly."

Tiffany hung up and eyed her sweatpants and tank top in a panic. She ran into the kitchen and turned the stove heat to low. Then she ran into the bathroom, freshened up and changed into a pair of jeans and a blouse.

Twenty minutes later, she was pulling the steaks out of the broiler when the doorbell rang.

A jolt of energy coursed through her veins. She walked to the door, ran her tongue over her teeth a final time, and opened it.

"Hi." Ivan smiled.

Tiffany stepped aside to let him enter. She shut the door, motioning for him to sit on the couch. She headed toward the kitchen.

"Make yourself at home. I'll be right back. Would you like some wine?"

"No, I'm good."

She stared at her glass longingly. She wanted to have one to settle her nerves more than anything, but she would wait.

"It'll be a few more minutes," she told him.

"You have a beautiful home."

"Thank you."

Ivan took a deep breath. "Tiffany, I don't want to be presumptuous, so if this is off base, tell me…but I think it's time to acknowledge that there's an attraction between us. At least that's what I took away from our actions at the seniors' class."

Tiffany wrapped her arms around her middle. "What actions?"

"Unless I missed the mark, we almost kissed. Didn't we?"

She could only manage a nod.

Ivan took a deep breath and continued. "I like you, Tiffany. A great deal, so I need to be honest with you about something. I—"

Unable to wait, she blurted out, "I already know you have a girlfriend, Ivan."

Ivan sat back. His expression relayed his surprise. "Did you say *girlfriend?*"

She nodded and went over to sit next to Ivan on the couch. "I know about Debra. I overheard you and Cole talking the day you installed my security system. I came back in to get my phone, and I didn't mean to eavesdrop, but I heard you discussing her—and..."

"And...you surmised that Debra and I are together?"

"Of course. You said she needed you, and that you made a promise to always be there for her. I'd say that speaks volumes."

"I guess it does," he replied.

"So it's obvious that you and I really should stop this before it goes any further. I'm sorry I got caught up in my...attraction to you. Or that I allowed myself to almost kiss you, but I assure you that I respect other women's relationships, and I truly apologize for my actions. It won't happen again."

"Good to know." He chuckled.

She lowered her gaze. He sounded almost relieved. It was a blow she found hard to recover from. Standing up, she said distractedly, "I'll go check on dinner."

Before Tiffany got farther than a foot, Ivan was in front of her.

"Tiffany, there are two things you need to know before we go out."

"Go out? Go out where?"

"On a date."

She stood there dumbfounded. "I don't… What are you talking about?"

"Tiffany, Debra is not my girlfriend."

She was still unable to process what he'd told her. "I don't understand. You said—"

"She and I are not together. She… It's a long story, but the short version is that she and I used to date about five years ago. I was deployed and only came home on leave. Debra decided that she didn't want to be an army wife. This caused serious tension in our relationship."

"Wife?" Tiffany repeated.

"Yes, we were talking about marriage at the time. Until I found out that she was dating a man on my team. She met him while he and I were on leave. I invited him to dinner at our house. Apparently there was a connection. When I found out that she was cheating on me—with him—let's just say I didn't take it well. I refused to play games or be in some love triangle. I left her and never looked back. He and I suffered a serious blow to our friendship. Six months later, they got married."

She nodded. "Whoa. How did you feel about that? Were you hurt?"

"Hell, yes. She says she doesn't want to be married to a military man, and then up and weds my teammate? That told me the real issue was that she didn't want to marry *me.* I won't lie, my pride was bruised—a lot—but I got over it. Her husband and I definitely had a strained relationship after that, but in our job, we had to rely on each other. Personal B.S. couldn't get in the way of our missions. The good of the team was always the top priority."

"So you sucked it up."

"Yeah, I did. Anyway, he died a year later. Took a bullet to the stomach. He didn't make it. I contacted Debra directly to let her know what happened. She didn't take the news well."

"Who would expect her to?"

"She blamed me for his death, and I can't fault her for that."

"Why?"

"It was my operation. I was in charge."

"But it wasn't your fault!" Tiffany grasped his hand. "You're not to blame, Ivan."

"Still, I promised him I'd make sure she would be okay. Brian had insurance, and Debra was entitled to military benefits. But it wasn't enough, and Debra wasn't working, so I stepped in to help."

"So that's what you and Cole were discussing when I overheard you."

"Yes. He thinks I should stop helping her financially, and continuing to do so sends the wrong message to her. Like there's a chance we'll get back together."

Tiffany searched his face. "Is there?"

"No. It was over the moment she cheated on me and didn't have the decency to end our relationship first," he said vehemently. "Make no mistake, I don't harbor any feelings for Debra, but I also don't wish her ill will. She's down right now, and I'm trying to help out. That's it."

"I hear what you're saying, and it's admirable you'd want to help her through a difficult time, but...does she still have feelings for you?"

"I can't answer that. I have no idea if she's hoping for more than my monetary support, but that's all I'm giving."

"And how long is that?"

"I don't know. Cole and my dad have been pretty vocal about their opinion. They think she's taking advantage of me."

"And what do you think?" she said quietly.

"I made a promise, Tiffany. I can't break it. That's not who I am."

She placed a hand on his shoulder. "I get it, but surely

you don't think it's feasible to help her indefinitely—do you?"

"Of course not. It was only until she got back on her feet."

"Maybe you should check in. You know, see how she's doing. Maybe she's already looking for a job."

Ivan nodded. His gaze held hers for several moments. Finally he said, "I will, but I don't want to talk about Debra anymore. There's something else you need to know."

With a deep breath, she said, "I'm listening."

He took her hand and held it suspended between them before he raised it to his lips and kissed it. He lowered it, but didn't let go.

"It was apparent to me after you left the community center the other day that I didn't make my intentions clear. I guess I'm out of practice, so let me rectify that oversight immediately. Tiffany, would you like to go out on a date with me tomorrow night?"

Tiffany could feel relief and then happiness flitter across her face.

"Yes," she replied. "I'd love to go out on a date with you—and I'm very glad you're single."

He grinned. "Does that mean you won't feel guilty the next time we almost kiss?"

"Who said I felt guilty?"

"Your face is very expressive."

"Okay, maybe I did feel guilty, but I don't now," she clarified.

"Good, because I've wanted to do something else since I arrived."

Before Tiffany could ask what, Ivan's lips descended on hers.

What started out as an exploratory kiss grew more intimate. He kissed her with a confidence, as though he'd done so a thousand times before. Then he tightened his hold to bring her closer still. It blew her mind.

Tiffany did what she had longed to do since the day she met him. She rubbed the back of his head with the palm of her hand. It was smooth, like she had imagined. Being in his arms, and knowing that she had every right to do so, produced a rush of adrenaline. Tiffany was so elated, she could hardly stand still.

Ivan broke their kiss and released her. "I'm sorry. I didn't mean to come on so strong, it's just that…I've thought of nothing else for a very, very long time."

Tiffany stared at him in wonder. "You didn't. I wasn't trying to get away." She laughed. "I was just…antsy. I think I've wanted to kiss you like that since the day we met."

"Me, too," he confessed. "You'd blush if you knew all the thoughts going through my head after that self-defense class."

Her smile was radiant. "Really?"

"Tiffany, do you have any idea how sexy you looked in your workout gear? After you left, the image was in my head the rest of that evening—and every evening since."

She wrapped her arms around his neck and brought his head down for another kiss, and reveled when she felt his arms encircle her waist to keep her close.

Tiffany headed to the kitchen and pulled Ivan along behind her. "My nerves are shot. You can't imagine all the things I thought you were going to tell me tonight."

"I'm sorry. I had no idea you thought Debra and I were together. No wonder you were worried."

"You don't know the half of it."

He tilted her face up to meet his. "I'm an idiot, and I plan on making it up to you."

"You do? How?"

"You'll see."

"Wait. It can't be tomorrow. We're due at the Andersons' house for a barbecue, remember?"

Ivan frowned. "Now I do. Well, how about Monday?"

"I'm free. So where are we going?"

"I'm not telling. It's a surprise."

"I hate surprises."

Ivan wrapped his arms around her waist and held her close. "Trust me, you'll love this one."

For the next hour, they camped out on the floor, talking and eating like they were at a real picnic. The more Tiffany learned about Ivan, the more she liked.

"I'm glad you came over," she told him. "For a lot of reasons."

His expression was playful. "Me, too."

They moved to the couch and watched a movie. When it was over, Ivan said, "I think it's time I said good-night. Thanks for having me over."

Tiffany walked him to the door. "You're welcome. I had a great time."

"Me, too."

When he left, Tiffany closed and locked the door.

With a high-wattage smile, she went back and flopped on the couch. "Well, that definitely wasn't my plan for tonight, but it sure as heck worked!"

Chapter 8

Norma Jean was setting her peach cobbler on top of the stove. She bent over to close the oven door.

"I didn't marry you for your cooking, but it's sure been an added bonus—one of them," her husband said from the doorway.

She beamed at the compliment. "Don't go trying to get a taste before the guests arrive—of anything."

Heathcliffe walked over and dipped his head to smell the delectable aroma. He kissed his wife on the neck. "I'm sure I don't know what you mean."

"Sure you don't. Remember, I'm watching you, Mr. Anderson."

"After all these years, it's great to know that you're still scoping me out."

Norma Jean swiped an oven mitt through the air in his direction, but her face was aglow. "Stop being fresh, Casanova."

"Anything for you, sexy."

"Okay, stop. You two had plenty of time to chase each other around before we got here," Adrian complained from behind them.

"Boy, please. This is my house, and I'll get fresh with whomever I choose," his mother replied.

"I'd better be the only one you're getting fresh with," her husband countered.

She smiled at him, and then turned her attention back to her son.

"Do I tell you what to do in your home? Lord knows I've had plenty of opportunities with the way you chase your wife through every room in your house."

Adrian grinned with a devilish glint in his eye. "Touché, Mom, but can you at least keep it to a minimum until after we leave?"

Norma Jean went over to give her husband a smooch on the lips before turning back to her son. "I might."

With a shudder, Adrian set the tote bag he was carrying on the table and took out a square covered dish. "Milán made flan, and it needs to go into the fridge."

"Great. Your hands aren't broke. Put it in there, and then get the burgers from the second shelf and take them outside for your father, please. Cliff, is the grill ready?"

He stared at her. "You wanted me to start that?"

Before Norma Jean could get riled up, her husband burst out laughing. "Just kidding, lovebug. It's all ready to go."

Milán walked through the door. She said hello to her in-laws. "Do you need me to carry anything out to the back? Tiffany's on her way around the side with a cooler."

Norma Jean went over and kissed her daughter-in-law on the cheek. "Yes, honey. Can you carry that tray of condiments to the deck? Where are Justin and Sabrina?"

"They couldn't make it," Adrian informed her. "They're on vacation."

"Oh. Well, I'm glad Tiffany's here."

The doorbell chimed. Norma Jean said, "You go on out, I'll get it."

Ivan stood on the front stoop with a roasting pan in his hands. "Did someone place an order for barbecue beans?"

"I sure did. Come on in, Ivan," she replied, and then kissed him on the cheek. "Everyone is out back."

Ivan followed her out to the deck. He set his contribution down on the table and greeted the group.

Tiffany waved and walked over to him. "Hi, Ivan, it's good to see you," she said.

They shared a secret smile before he said, "Likewise."

"Where's your brother?"

"He's in Evanston visiting our grandmother."

"You'll have to take him a doggie bag," Milán said, coming over to greet him.

The group conversed while eating the snacks Norma Jean had prepared. Heathcliffe worked the grill, and his son supervised.

"You do know that I've been the Grill Master in this family since before you were born," his father told him. "It's not like anyone has developed an advanced way of flipping burgers that I don't know about."

"As a matter of fact, they have. It's called the rocker technique. You have to get your hip into it and then rock back on your heels and then forward before you flip the meat." Adrian demonstrated the move.

His father laughed. "Thanks, but I think my tried-and-true method will be fine."

"There's no way you're getting that spatula, Adrian," Tiffany said.

"My father won't give up his, either," Ivan joined in. "My brother and I can't grill so much as an ear of corn when he's around."

"Like it should be," Heathcliffe replied. "You young

bucks get the honors when you're at your own house. Then you can be Grill Master, and us dads can sit and relax."

When the meat was ready, they sat down at the large table set up on the lawn. Heathcliffe blessed the food, and then dishes and plates were passed around.

"The food looks delicious," he complimented his wife. "As always."

The group seconded that motion, and Norma Jean beamed with pride.

"I'm glad to do it, and thank you, dears, for bringing such wonderful dishes, too."

Tiffany was sitting across from Ivan. She took a bite of his beans and exclaimed, "Wow. What's in these beans? It's like a meal on its own."

"Thanks. It's my dad's recipe. It has hamburger, green pepper, onions, a few different barbecue sauces and some secret ingredients."

Norma Jean glanced over at Tiffany. "So I hear you've been holding out on me."

Tiffany was taking a bite out of her burger when suddenly all eyes were on her. "I have?"

"I heard that you helped Ivan with his senior self-defense class the other day. A few of my friends were in the class and said that you were terrific."

Her face was flushed with embarrassment at being called out in front of everyone…especially Ivan. She remembered their almost kiss that night. Thank goodness they hadn't been caught making out, or Norma Jean definitely would have gotten an earful. She wondered what she would say if she knew about their impromptu date at her house the night before. Though Tiffany wasn't looking directly at Ivan, she could still feel the heat of his gaze. It was boring into her like a laser beam. There was no way she was going to risk gazing into those tiger eyes right now. Not when she felt like a gazelle caught between the tiger and a hard place.

"Uh, well…it wasn't at all what I expected. I didn't think I would be any good at demonstrating the moves since they were new to me, but Ivan is a great teacher, and it went much better than I expected."

"That's great, honey." She turned to Ivan. "I hope you plan on having Tiffany help out with class again. The group enjoyed having her there."

"I did, too. She's a natural. She caught on to my techniques in record time."

Tiffany's breath caught in her throat at being reminded of their conversation about his techniques. Unable to help herself, she raised her head and was not surprised to find Ivan staring right at her. He definitely looked like a tiger ready to pounce.

If anyone noticed the smoldering heat between the two of them, nobody mentioned it. Heathcliffe began talking about how much he liked water aerobics and how good it was for his joints. Norma Jean chimed in about the class she taught, and chastised her husband for never taking it, but Tiffany didn't hear either of them. She only had eyes for Ivan.

"I get bossed around by you at home, Jeannie. The last thing I want to do is have you giving me orders in a class," Heathcliffe groused.

Tiffany was grateful that the awkward moment passed, and that she was no longer the center of conversation. She excused herself and left the table under the guise of going to the bathroom. Once there, she shut the door and sank against it. Her heart was racing, and her stomach tingled from nervous energy.

Relax, her inner voice instructed.

Tiffany tried hard to steady her breathing. There was no way she could go out there right now. All Ivan would have to do was look at her with those smoldering eyes again, and she would lose her composure for sure.

Suddenly there was a knock at the door.

"Hey, it's me. Open up," her friend whispered through the door. "Are you okay?" she asked with concern.

"I'm fine," Tiffany replied. "Be out in a minute."

Tiffany rushed over to the sink and splashed cold water on her face. She repeated the action, and then grabbed a hand towel and patted her face dry. "Get a grip, girl. It's not like drop-dead gorgeous men have never eyed you like you were candy before."

She laughed at that and left the bathroom, and then went back outside. Dinner was over, so they all helped bring the dishes inside.

"How about dessert?" Milán asked when the kitchen was clean. "We've got Jeannie's famous peach cobbler, Tiffany made key-lime pie, and I made flan."

They ate dessert in the Cupid Room, Adrian's nickname for the family room. It had white carpet and walls, and neutral chenille couches, but that was where the lack of color ended. Every surface in the room was dedicated to romance: books, stuffed animals, candles, paintings, photo albums. Adrian joked to Ivan that it looked like a love bomb went off in there.

Tiffany found herself sandwiched between Norma Jean and Ivan. Instead of her own pie, she opted for small pieces of cobbler and flan. She was taking a bite of cobbler when Ivan leaned in and whispered into her ear, "Your key-lime pie was delicious."

"Thank you," Tiffany replied, almost choking on her dessert.

"Do you bake much?"

She shook her head. "Not really. I like sweets way, way too much to make them often."

"So why did you disappear so long after dinner that Milán had to come in after you?"

The hairs on the back of her neck stood up as his warm breath tickled her ear.

"No reason."

"I have a feeling you're leaving some things out."

"Oh, really?" she murmured. "And how would you know?"

"I'm good at figuring out when people are telling the truth, and when they're being…purposefully deceptive."

"Something you picked up in the army?"

"Yes."

That answer relayed Ivan's confidence and abilities, and hinted at something else she could not put her finger on. Her palms grew sweaty.

"I'm not being deceptive," she whispered, and then got up and headed for the kitchen.

Ivan joined her a minute later. His eyes searched her face.

"Are you sure you're okay?"

"Yeah."

"Your eyes say differently."

"Tiffany, do we have any—"

Milán scooted to a halt when she saw that her friend wasn't alone. "Iced tea left?"

"I put it in the fridge," Tiffany replied.

"Um, thanks."

Walking to the refrigerator, Milán got what she needed. She stared at Tiffany with a questioning look on her face. Tiffany smiled, and her friend relaxed.

"I'll take this in to Adrian," she explained before hurrying out of the room.

Tiffany wasn't surprised in the least to find that Ivan hadn't moved an inch during that exchange. He was still ramrod-straight, and staring at her.

"You must be proficient at interrogating people," she joked. "Okay. I give. I came in to get away from the conversation at dinner. It was…uncomfortable for me."

"Why?"

"Because Norma Jean misses nothing, and I didn't want her picking up on what's between us."

"And what is between us, Tiffany?"

"Sometimes, I think, way too much space."

In a split second, Tiffany was in his arms in an embrace that left little to the imagination. His lips swept over hers possessively, as did his hands. Just when she was getting caught up in the moment, he released her.

Tiffany staggered backward. Ivan reached out and steadied her. "Let's get out of here. I want you all to myself."

She nodded. He kissed her a final time before releasing her. Ivan strode out of the kitchen, leaving Tiffany holding onto the sink for dear life. When she could stand, she ran a shaky hand through her spiked hair. "Heaven help me."

Chapter 9

Tiffany didn't know how she managed it, but she had stayed at the Andersons' all of five minutes after she came out of the kitchen. No one questioned her leaving. Not even Norma Jean. She roamed around her house, at a loss for something to do. Ivan had already texted that he was on his way. She went to the kitchen and got a bottle of wine and two wineglasses. Next she put together a small plate of cheese, crackers and grapes. She had just placed it on the coffee table when her doorbell rang.

Seeing Ivan never failed to bring a smile to her face.

"Hi."

"Hi, yourself," he replied before kissing her.

"You didn't stay long," she commented as she stepped aside so he could enter.

"Nope."

They sat on her couch. Tiffany poured a glass of wine for each of them and handed one to Ivan. He held his glass up.

"To evasive maneuvers."

She laughed and clinked his glass. "Are you sure Norma Jean didn't suspect anything? She misses nothing."

"I'm very good at covering my tracks. Trust me, the Love Broker doesn't suspect a thing," Ivan promised.

Later that night, Ivan was lying in bed with his laptop when he got a call from his brother.

"What's up, Cole?"

"Hey, I'm downtown at the Funky Buddha Lounge with a few friends. Why don't you join me?"

Ivan was not big on crowds. "It's Sunday night."

"So?"

"Don't you have work tomorrow?"

"Yes, but unlike you, I can go out on a school night and still get my work done. Come on, Ivan. You haven't gone out on the town in decades. Swipe one of Dad's energy drinks from the fridge and get down here."

He had to laugh at that. "No can do. I'm going out to dinner tomorrow, and I'm trying to pick a restaurant."

"Oh, make sure you tell GiGi I said hi."

"It's not with our grandmother," Ivan said drily.

"Come again?"

"I'm going out with Tiffany."

"You're going out…on a date…with Tiffany?" Cole repeated loudly.

The incredulous tone in Cole's voice irritated Ivan. "Yes, we're going out," he snapped. "And before you ask, yes, I finally told her about Debra."

"And she still wants to go out with you?"

Ivan ignored that remark.

"So where are you taking her?"

He frowned. "I'm not sure yet. I was working on it when you called."

"Wherever it is better be good. This woman wants to

be with you, despite your nonsense with Debra. That says a lot."

"It's not nonsense."

"Yeah, whatever. How many people do you know who fund a friend's widow for as long as you have? I'll tell you. Zilch, that's how many."

"It hasn't been that long, Cole, and it's not permanent."

"Most disasters aren't. You've done a noble thing. Now it's time for Debra to stand on her own two feet."

After Cole hung up, Ivan dismissed his concerns. He'd sort all that out later. Right now, he wanted to focus on Tiffany. The last time he was on a date was over a year ago. A client call had cut it short. There had not been a second one. At times, Ivan's schedule was unpredictable, and that tended to be hard on his love life.

He thought back to the conversation with his grandmother. She was right. He was stuck in a rut. A large part of him enjoyed his regimented life. There was a comfort in the predictability of it. Adjusting to civilian life hadn't been without its difficulties, but his line of work afforded the same rigid conditioning and procedural aspects that he was used to. Being his own boss enabled him to hire retired veterans and honorably discharged servicemen and women, and it also gave him the means to lend his time, money and support to causes and charities he felt passionate about. There was no better feeling.

Looking for a meaningful relationship took time, and that was a commodity Ivan had little of. But business was going well, and his company was stable. Other than the occasional fire to put out, for the immediate future, he had nothing but time. Ivan went back to searching for a suitable restaurant. Should he go for something hip and trendy, or more laid-back with ambience?

Ivan thought about Tiffany for a moment and what little he knew about her. His brow furrowed with concentration as he scanned websites and reviews. One particular place caught his eye. He glanced over the pictures, and then read each evaluation.

"Perfect."

He wanted his first date with Tiffany to be extraordinary. Based on what he had gleaned so far, too many of her dates fell short of the mark. Ivan did not intend to be one of those.

"So, how was your evening with Ivan?"

If Milán could see her face right now, she would not have to ask. "Why do you think I was with Ivan?"

"Let's see, you leave the barbecue minutes after your secret meeting in the kitchen, claiming you have to get into work early today, and he spent the remainder of his time after you left checking his watch—then hightails it out of there a short time later. Real subtle, Tiffy."

"First of all, it wasn't secret…" she began.

Milán broke into a litany of Spanish so fast, it made Tiffany dizzy.

"Okay, okay," she cried out to stop the tirade. "Yes, I was with Ivan last night, and the night before. He asked me out on a date, Lani!"

After letting out a whoop, Milán congratulated her friend. "So what happened?"

"A great deal." She sighed. "He's taking me out tonight."

"I'm so happy for you, but you're in trouble for not telling me sooner."

"I'm sorry, it's just been so crazy."

"I can't believe you even made it in to work today. Do you have any idea what you're wearing tonight?"

"No clue. But I'm excited to figure it out."

The morning went by in record time for Tiffany, which was a blessing in disguise because she could not stop smiling, and concentration was a pipe dream. It was a good thing she was scheduled to work most of the day by herself, or else she would've gotten the third degree from her employees. As it turned out, they were swamped that afternoon. Tiffany barely made it home to shower and dress before Ivan was due to pick her up.

Should she dress up, or keep it casual? She had no idea the type of venue Ivan had in mind, and she didn't want to call and ask.

Finally Tiffany chose a sleeveless, knee-length crochet dress in coral. The vibrant color and matching underdress complemented her complexion. She paired it with a pair of beige platform sandals and small gold hoop earrings. She set her hair on end with styling mousse before spraying it with a light mist of hair spray. Satisfied with the look, she applied her makeup.

Tiffany was no stranger to first dates, but she knew off the bat that this one would be nerve-racking. What if things didn't work out? What if they weren't compatible after all?

Fifteen minutes later, her doorbell rang. Ivan stood there holding a small bag.

"What's that?" Tiffany asked.

"A little something I saw and thought of you."

She sat on the couch to open it while Ivan took a seat on the chair. Tiffany peeked into the bag. "I can't believe you did this. It's not even my birthday."

Ivan shook his head. "Will you open your gift?"

In the small bag, she maneuvered around loads of tissue paper to pull out a pink T-shirt. It had *Girl Power* written in bold letters across the front.

"I thought it would be great to wear for our next class."

"Our next class?"

"You didn't think I could do without you as an assistant, did you?" he said seriously. "You're a natural."

She laughed. "It's awesome, I love it."

Tiffany leaned over and kissed him. The light peck went from friendly to something deeper in seconds.

Ivan stood up and pulled her with him. Tiffany wrapped her arms around his neck. His automatically went to her waist to bring her closer.

"Okay, we need to get going," he said when they came up for air.

"Why?"

"We have reservations, and I don't want to be known as the man who tried to ravage you on the first date. Though I really do feel the need to do just that," he replied wickedly before kissing her a final time.

Now that they'd cleared the air about Debra, Ivan had officially asked her out on a date and they had shared a few heated kisses, Tiffany was overwhelmed with want. It felt like a floodgate had opened, and there was no chance in the world of closing it. She wanted Ivan before, and knowing that he felt the same was intoxicating.

She ran her thumb over his lips to remove her lipstick. He caught her wrist in a firm embrace and pulled her flush against him.

"That's dangerous," he warned.

"I know, but I've wanted to touch you for so long, I couldn't help myself."

His eyes darkened. "Really?" A feral smile came across his face. "For how long?"

She didn't hesitate. "Since you walked through my door wearing that tight Under Armour shirt."

"I've wanted you ever since our meeting at the café. You straddling me on the floor at the community center was the icing on the cake."

"I didn't straddle you," she protested.

"Oh, yes, you did," he teased. "Not that I minded in the least."

She punched his arm, but a smile crossed her face.

After taking her gift into the bedroom and returning with her purse and a wrap, Tiffany said she was ready.

Ivan sauntered over to her, placed his hand at the small of her back and escorted her out.

"Did I mention that you look beautiful tonight?"

She couldn't contain her smile at remembering how he had told her. "Yes, I'd say you did."

Ivan was wearing all black. He looked gorgeous.

"You look great yourself."

He leaned in close. His breath tickled her ear. "You told me."

Ivan took Tiffany to Spiaggia on Michigan Avenue. She had heard about the acclaimed restaurant, but had never been. While they were shown to their table, Tiffany gazed around. The space was ultraluxurious and beautifully decorated. Ivan held out her chair. Their table was right next to a massive floor-to-ceiling window, which afforded a spectacular view of Oak Street Beach.

"This place is phenomenal," she said excitedly. "If I'd known we were coming here, I would've dressed up more."

"You look beautiful."

She beamed at the compliment and tried her best to focus on the menu, and not the man sitting across from her. It was so hard when he gazed at her like that.

Ivan had spared no expense for their first date, and she allowed herself to enjoy every decadent moment of it.

Later, while they were eating, Ivan said, "So I know you're from Baltimore, an only child and that you moved here to a few years ago for a job, but what made you move to Chicago in the first place?"

"I needed a change. There was no room for growth at the marketing firm I worked at. I looked around for another position, but nothing seemed to excite me. I was also having difficulties with my boyfriend. I wasn't as sure of myself—or my abilities."

"I have a hard time believing that."

"It's true. I worked hard to overcome it. The decision to move here was one of the hardest I've ever made, but when I got an offer to work at this small boutique to head up their marketing campaign, I took that as a sign that I needed to shake things up."

"Did your boyfriend relocate with you?"

Her smile faded. "No. His career was flourishing. Uprooting to another state wasn't one of his long-term goals. So that was that. I should've seen it coming."

"Why?"

"We'd been engaged for two years, but never set a date. The timing was always wrong, as far as he was concerned. It took me a while, but eventually I realized that we weren't of the same mind. Breaking up was painful. It broke my heart, and made me doubt myself. There were times when…secretly, I hoped we would get back together. That he would call me or just show up here to say he'd made a huge mistake and that he wanted us to try again, but that never happened. He never fought for me…for us." She glanced over at Ivan with eyes alight with unshed tears. "You must think that's pretty silly."

He reached for her hand. "Not at all. I understand how in love you must've been, and that your decision to move on even though you still loved him was extremely difficult. Not wanting the same things in life is what ripped to shreds most of the relationships I've had—that and my being so far away. Believe me, Tiffany, I know exactly how you feel."

Tiffany dabbed at the corner of her eyes with her dinner napkin before taking a sip of her wine. "Okay, enough melancholy."

"I agree. Tell me about your store. How'd you get started?"

"Well, I wasn't fulfilled working for someone else, and

when Milán opened her own interior-design company, that gave me the incentive I needed to get off my butt and make things happen. My grandmother left me a small nest egg when she died a few years ago, so that's what I used to help get my boutique off the ground. That and a small business loan," she added. "But I did it."

"I commend you for taking a chance and starting a small business. You had the gumption to realize your dreams, and you went for it."

"What about you? How did you get your company started?"

"I began consulting after I ended my last tour and got out of the army. I decided not to reinvent the wheel as far as a career, and stuck with security and protection. It expanded from there, and I soon realized it was a lucrative market. I brought a few retired buddies in with me, and the company grew exponentially. But you know what I love most about it?"

She shook her head.

"It still fills me with a sense of accomplishment, and it makes me proud to be able to continue making a difference in people's lives."

Tiffany held up her glass. "Here's to us. May we never lose sight of dreams and what makes us truly fulfilled."

Ivan held up his glass and clinked it with hers. "Here's to you, for having such an antiquated alarm system that allowed us to meet in the first place."

That made her laugh. She touched his glass again, and took a sip of her wine. "You don't think Norma Jean would've eventually tried to push us together? Granted, you're built like a tank, so I really don't think anyone would be pushing you too far, but if anyone could, it would be Jeannie."

Ivan's right eyebrow shot up. "A tank?"

"Yes, a devastatingly handsome, incredibly sexy tank," she added.

"Oh, well, then I can deal with tank." He grinned lasciviously. "And no, I don't think she would've tried matching us up. I was pretty clear when I told her I wasn't interested in blind dates. So far she's respected my wishes."

Tiffany looked skeptical. "About as clear as Adrian has been over the last twenty years?"

"Well, he's her son. Of course she has a vested interest in him marrying."

They both had a good laugh at that. Since Ivan was relatively new to the Love Broker experience, Tiffany brought him up to speed on some of her not-so-near misses.

"I think you all should find Jeannie a new hobby. It doesn't sound like she's that great a matchmaker."

"I wonder about that," Tiffany said seriously. "I think she's shrewder than anybody gives her credit for."

Ivan glanced up from his plate. "How so?"

"Think about it. She sets up all these dates that go awry, and when a real connection is made, it's like fireworks, and all the past nightmares make couples appreciate when it goes right. You don't think that's like reverse psychology or something?"

Ivan pondered that for a moment. "Nah. Jeannie didn't have anything to do with Adrian and Milán getting together. She introduced them for business reasons, and then they found their way on their own."

Tiffany was speculative. "Or did they?"

After dinner, they shared a torta al ricotta e mascarpone for dessert.

"Okay, I'm seriously done," she groaned after taking the last bite. "I can't thank you enough for bringing me here, Ivan. It was the best Italian I've ever had."

Ivan paid the bill and then helped her up. "I'm glad you liked it."

When they got outside, Ivan had the valet bring his Range Rover around.

He checked his watch. "I've got an idea for what we can do now, but we have to hurry."

Ivan drove them the short distance to Navy Pier, a Chicago tradition for entertainment and summer fun on Lake Michigan since its revitalization years before. The landmark had over fifty acres of gardens, promenades, restaurants, shops and attractions.

"Where are we going?" she asked. "If you think I'm going on a hundred-and-fifty-foot-high Ferris wheel after eating all that food, think again."

"That's not what we're doing."

Tiffany took a moment to ogle the forty spokes of the ride lit up in sparkling lights. "It's beautiful."

Ivan stopped to grab her hand. "It is, but keep moving."

"We aren't going to ride the carousel, or the wave swinger, are we?"

"I promise that you won't be going on anything motorized."

They reached the dock, where Tiffany was afforded a beautiful view of the water and the surrounding sites.

"It's so lovely at night, isn't it? I've often wished that—"

Tiffany halted when she saw the first fireworks burst overhead, followed by loud claps and applause.

"Oh, my gosh," she exclaimed excitedly. "I forgot about the fireworks."

"Two nights a week during the summer, and lucky for us, we're here at the right time." He put an arm around her and eased her into his side.

"I will give you one thing, Colonel Mangum," she said over the racket. "When you take a girl out, you go all in."

"Go hard or go home," he said with a grin. "Words I live by."

After a loud cheer at the latest light display, she said, "I can see that."

By the time they arrived back at her apartment, Tiffany was still wired. On the doorstep, Ivan wrapped his arms around her waist, and then reeled her in. He bent his head and claimed her mouth for a searing kiss. Tiffany wrapped her arms around his neck to get even closer. They parted a few seconds later, their breathing labored.

"This was an incredible night, and the best first date I've had."

"Me, too," she confessed. "Of course, I would've said that no matter where we ended up, because the best thing about my date was you."

"I agree." He grinned.

They shared another kiss, then he opened the front door and stepped into the corridor. "I'll see you later."

"Call me when you get home so that I know you're safe," she commanded. "I take my watch seriously, too."

With a grin, Ivan nodded. "I will."

Tiffany watched him until he was out of sight, then locked the door.

"Ivan Mangum," she purred. "You were definitely worth the wait."

Chapter 10

I swear next time he kisses me, the clothes are coming off. Just seeing Ivan saunter through the door of her shop each time was enough to make Tiffany giddy. It was like he had a direct line to her libido, and he never failed to get it pumping. Between helping Ivan with self-defense classes at the community center and their dates, they saw each other on a regular basis. That suited her just fine because she never tired of being around him—or looking at him.

She attempted to quell her sporadic breathing when their gazes connected from across the room. "Hi," she called out.

"Hey, yourself. How's your day been?"

"Great. I had a lovely group of ladies from a book club come in. It seems one of their members had on a shirt she bought from me. They liked it so much, they all decided to come in and get one. Isn't that fantastic?"

Ivan leaned over and kissed her. "Way to go. Do you have time for a break?"

"For you, I might."

They walked to the coffeehouse. Both ordered vanilla-bean frappés. It was a lovely day out, so Tiffany suggested they sit outside.

"So what's up?" she asked after a minute of companionable silence.

"I have to go out of town on assignment."

"Okay, where to?"

"Venice."

"How come you get to go to all the supercool places? What happened to guarding some insurance salesman going to the Ramada Inn in Hackensack, New Jersey?"

"None called."

"Fine." She laughed. "How long will you be gone?"

"A week."

She leaned forward. "I'll miss you."

Ivan kissed her. "How much?"

"More than you know. The Love Broker is having a Fourth of July party at her house on Saturday. We were invited," she informed him.

"Damn, I forgot all about that." He groaned. "I can't make it. I have another assignment—in Las Vegas. It's just overnight, though. I'll let her know today. She's going to kill me for not responding to her invitation sooner."

"You'd better do it before you leave," Tiffany warned. "You're coming back on Sunday, right?"

"Yep."

"Then, we'll go over then. She's having her usual Sunday night dinner."

"Two parties in a row? Isn't that a bit much, even for Jeannie?"

"Yes, but she insisted on doing both."

"Okay. I'll phone her on the way home. How about dinner tonight?"

She frowned. "I can't. I'm doing inventory later."

"What about tomorrow?"

"I don't know. I'll have to consult my calendar, Colonel Mangum. I can't be—"

Ivan silenced her with his lips. He was thorough in his assault, and when he pulled away, Tiffany almost went with him. She sat back slowly and said with considerable effort, "I'm free on Friday."

He gave her a smug look. "Great. How about seven o'clock at my place?"

"Your place? Uh, yeah. You certainly don't think I'm going to turn down an invitation to see where you live, do you? I was starting to think that it was some mythical place where unicorns and leprechauns lived."

"Funny," he countered. "We've got it back to a place where my mother won't kill me for having you over. She's old-school. She doesn't think of having company if the house doesn't look one hundred percent."

"I can understand that," Tiffany replied. "I'll be there at seven on Friday."

"We'll be there," he informed her. "I'm picking you up."

"Ivan, you don't have to come get me. I can drive myself."

"I know, but I'm picking you up anyway—if you have no objections, of course."

Tiffany started to protest, but then stopped. "I'll be awaiting my limo and driver."

He winked. "I also do private parties…if you're interested."

"Oh, I'm definitely interested," she replied, and then stared him up and down. She licked her lips for effect.

"Flirt."

Tiffany smiled. "I've got to get back to work, but I'm glad you told me about the trip." She stood up and held her hand out. "I'll miss you."

Ivan got up and slipped her hand in his. "I'll miss you too, Tiff."

They walked back to her store hand in hand. He kissed her a final time before he left.

Later that afternoon, Tiffany was at the table in the back room, working on her latest jewelry design. She had pages splayed out in front of her and was deep in concentration when Milán burst into the room. She spoke in rapid Spanish.

Tiffany stared back. "What?"

"I saw you and Ivan," Milán translated. "At the café. You two had your lips locked so tight, I thought you'd have to be separated by a surgical procedure."

"You're dramatizing it," Tiffany said, but couldn't help the blush that crept up her neck and face.

Milán observed her for a moment. "I knew it. You like him, don't you…a lot."

She set her sketches aside and turned in her chair. "That obvious?"

"Hmm…only a lot." Milán sat down next to her.

"I do like him—a lot," Tiffany admitted. "Ivan's an amazing guy. Granted, he's reserved, but he's intelligent, strong, protective and caring. Do you know how many languages he speaks? It's insane. He's a real gentleman, too. Though I have to admit, I'm trying to get used to a few things."

"Like what?"

"For one, the whole overprotective thing. He wants to do everything for me—pick me up, drop me off, hold my door. Do you know when we go out together, he comes back and does a sweep of my apartment to make sure it's safe?"

"Some might call that romantic," Milán observed.

"Yes, but he does it *all* the time."

"You're important to him, Tiff. So he goes a little overboard sometimes. What's wrong with that?"

She shook her head. "Nothing. It's just that…I'd like to still do things for myself sometimes."

"I get it. You haven't been spoiled like this before. It

takes some getting used to. It was the same with Adrian and me. He's so attentive now that it can be overwhelming."

Tiffany threw her hands up. "Exactly. Most of the time I do like him taking care of me. But I don't want to lose myself, you know? I've seen it happen before, and when things don't work out, it always ends badly."

"Stop imagining bumps in the road that aren't there," her friend chided. "You just got together. It's still new and exciting."

"I know. I'm so happy with Ivan, I really am."

"So his rock-hard body and physical stamina must seem like icing on the cake."

Tiffany dissolved into laughter before she sighed dreamily and said, "And what a cake he is!"

"Will Ivan be at the party next week?" Milán asked.

"No, he'll be in Vegas."

"Wow, what a life."

"Remember that he's often in danger of being shot at, or else he has to fight someone to protect his client. And don't forget all the time spent waiting around for people. Scoping out routes, times and tactical plans—"

"Or the hours standing around in posh clubs, driving expensive cars, going to exotic locales…looking dark and mysterious…in Armani," Milán said breathlessly.

Tiffany stared at her. "You're not helping."

"Okay, okay. I'm going, but you'd better not slip up on Saturday, or Jeannie will know you've been holding out. Starting with that ridiculous smile on your face."

"It's the same one you had for weeks after you and Adrian got together," Tiffany pointed out.

"Touché," her friend said, and then waved goodbye.

Tiffany sighed, and then grudgingly returned to her designs.

"So have you had sex yet?"

Ivan and Cole were in the exercise room lifting weights.

Ivan set his weights down with a bang, and glared at his brother.

"What? Can't a guy ask a question?"

"Sure," Ivan replied. "Just not one that involves my sex life."

"Since when?"

"Cole."

"Okay, okay."

"She's coming over on Friday. Are you going to be here?"

Cole looked up. "Now I am. So things are going well?"

Ivan began bench-pressing weights. "Yes. I enjoy being around her. She's smart, funny and talented. There's a lot packed into that petite body of hers."

"I guess you'll know that soon enough." He smirked.

Ivan sat up and scowled at his brother. "Don't make me deck you."

Cole started moving around and shadowboxing. "As if you could. You don't want any of this, old man."

"Anytime, little brother."

"All joking aside, I can see that she makes you happy. Personally, I think it's long overdue. I was starting to worry about your being married to your job. Which, dear brother, is just sad."

"Be quiet, and yes, Tiffany makes me happy. I like that she's independent and can hold her own. She's not intimidated by me in any way, so I don't feel the need to hold back. She's not forcing me to be something I'm not. I'm appreciative of that fact that I can be myself around Tiffany. The real me."

"I'm happy for you, but can she handle your work life? You travel often, and sometimes for long periods of time. It takes a strong woman to be able to handle coming in second to your career."

"I hear you, but Tiffany is a business owner, too. She's used to giving her all for her company."

"So, any word from Debra recently?"

"No."

"Have you told her about Tiffany?"

"Why should I? Debra and I have no romantic ties. I don't ask details of her personal life, and she doesn't ask about mine."

"She may not ask, Ivan," Cole countered, "but that doesn't mean she isn't interested."

"You're reading way more into this than necessary, little brother."

"Somebody has to. You're walking around under the illusion that it's rosy in Sunnyville. Need I remind you that this woman cheated on you with one of your army buddies, and ended up marrying him?"

Ivan picked up a barbell. "I let that go a long time ago. It's ancient history."

"Hey, I hope you're right. I'd hate to see her throw a monkey wrench in your program."

Ivan set the weight down and glanced over at Cole. "What is with you? You're like the poster child of partying and good times, and now all of a sudden you're big with the doom and gloom."

"I don't know," his brother replied. "I just have a good memory, and I know what her deception did to you. I'm not a big fan of second chances when someone rips your heart out—especially my flesh and blood. I don't want her getting an opportunity to do it again."

"Trust me, Debra has no bearing on what I do, and never will."

Ivan said goodbye to Cole and went upstairs to take a shower, Cole's words replaying in his head. His brother was right—sometimes stuff invariably came back to bite people in the butt later, but he felt sure this wasn't one of those times. The only thing he felt for Debra was empathy. Brian's death had hit him hard. He could only imagine what she was going through. Still, he was a realist. He wasn't a big fan of allowing someone to wreak havoc on his heart, and Debra had done just that. There would never be a second chance to screw him over.

"Never going to happen," Ivan said confidently.

Tiffany hated doing inventory. She glanced up at the clock. It was almost ten. She'd promised herself that she wouldn't leave until she was finished. She eyed her cell phone. She longed to call Ivan. He had been on her mind all night. Talking to Milán had stirred the already simmering embers into a full-out fire. Closing her eyes, she imagined he was touching and kissing her in all the right places. Frustrated, she opened her eyes.

Ivan. You're killing me.

With a reluctant sigh, Tiffany turned her attention back to work. It was too easy to get distracted, and any thoughts with Ivan as the subject were most definitely a distraction.

Chapter 11

Have you had sex yet? Ivan could kill his brother for making him painfully aware that he would like nothing more than to be buried to the hilt inside Tiffany, as opposed to listening to his travel agent drone on. He had been thinking about her ever since his conversation with Cole. The energy Tiffany exuded was almost tangible. He missed her when she wasn't around: her infectious laughter, her caring nature and her amazing body were the perfect trifecta for him. Soon his mind conjured up the things he would rather be doing—with her.

It had a domino effect. The more his employee talked, the more fidgety he became. Ivan prided himself on his ability to concentrate on the job at hand, but he'd reached his limit. The overwhelming urge to see Tiffany was too strong to ignore.

He wrapped up his conversation in record time, and changed from the pair of shorts he'd been wearing to an all-black jogging suit. He retrieved his wallet, keys and cell phone from his nightstand and ran down the stairs.

"Where you off to?" Cole asked from his spot on the couch.

"Just going to check up on Tiffany," he replied without stopping.

Cole smiled knowingly as Ivan left the house.

He got into his truck and headed straight for the boutique. Tiffany mentioned doing inventory. He hoped that she was still there. When he arrived at her store, he drove slowly past her window. There was no one in the front, but the lights were still on. Parking the SUV across the street, Ivan got out and strode over to the store. He knocked several times before Tiffany came out of the back room. Cautiously, she approached the door. When she saw him, she grinned and unlocked it.

"Hi," was all she managed to get out before Ivan scooped her up and kissed her. She wrapped her legs around his waist and ran her hands through his hair. He pushed the door shut with his back and then rested against it, never once breaking contact with her lips. Eventually, he turned around so that Tiffany was against the door, allowing him better access to kiss her neck and collarbone.

"Ivan," Tiffany moaned. "What if someone walks by?"

"They'll get a show," he responded in a voice laden with need.

Moments later, he carried her through the store and into the break room. He placed her on the nearest table and continued his torturous exploration.

He raised her shirt up to rain kisses from her belly upward. When he reached her breasts, he kissed the top of each before he skimmed his hand over the silky material encasing them.

His amber eyes glowed with desire and purpose, as he nibbled her neck and ears, and then recaptured her mouth.

Never had he felt such a blinding need before. It caused his body to vibrate with an unrivaled longing to possess her. Hearing her whimpers of pleasure only increased his appetite. He wanted more. He wanted all of Tiffany, but a romp on a store table wouldn't cut it.

Ivan broke their kiss and stared down at Tiffany. She was disheveled, flushed and had never looked sexier.

"Hi," he said raggedly.

He helped her up and gently adjusted her clothing with unsteady hands. She was just as affected, holding on to his shoulders for stability. After a few deep breaths, Tiffany ran a hand through her hair.

"What was that?"

Ivan wasn't ready to break contact with her. He touched his hand to her arm, following the planes of her body up to cup her jaw. He struggled with the burning urge to sample her all over again.

"I…had an overwhelming desire to see you. I hope I didn't scare you. Honestly, I don't know what came over me."

She bit her lower lip. "Well, whatever it was, I liked it—a lot."

"You did?"

She ran her hand up his chest. "Heck, yeah. It was…an unexpected pleasure."

"In that case, you should know that I didn't want to stop."

"Me, either," Tiffany confessed.

He traced a finger down her neck and across the scoop in her shirt. "As much as I wanted to make love to you right here on this table, I think our first time together should be on a surface a lot more comfortable."

"I agree. I'm glad you came to see me, though. I was hoping you would."

He kissed the palm of her hand. "You want me to help?"

"That would make this go faster."

"I'm at your command, milady."

"Really?" she asked boldly.

Ivan cupped her rear end. "Don't push your luck, or we'll finish what we started, and table be damned."

They worked well together, finishing up her inventory in less than an hour. Ivan helped her lock up afterward.

He walked her back to her car. "I'll follow you home."

Tiffany didn't bother telling him that she was fine and didn't need an escort. Granted, Ivan was a little overprotective, but it wasn't worth getting into a disagreement about it. They were just getting used to each other. Pretty soon, he wouldn't be so attentive, she reasoned. In truth, Tiffany was just happy to be able spend more time with him.

When she got home, she parked her car, and then Ivan escorted her inside. He performed his usual check of her apartment while she waited in the foyer.

"Do you have to do that every time?"

"I feel better when I do," he confessed. "Does it bother you?"

A part of her wanted to tell him yes, but instead she said, "No, of course not."

She set her purse down on the table. "What a night." She sighed.

"I don't like you being at the store so late by yourself."

"Ivan, I'm perfectly fine. You installed my security system, and I double-check to make sure my doors are always locked at closing. I'm good."

He held out his hand. "Come here for a minute."

She walked over. "What's wrong?"

Ivan performed a series of movements in the air in front of her so fast that she could barely keep up.

"What was that?" she said in wonder.

"Three strikes you can use in close proximity to render an attacker defenseless. It's what I'd planned to go over in the next class. I want you to get proficient in these moves—just in case."

He walked her through blows to the groin, solar plexus and the tip of the chin.

"Now you try," he instructed.

He let Tiffany move through the exercises, and coached her until her speed improved.

Ivan went to grab her wrists. Without hesitation, Tiffany escaped and caught him with a blow to the stomach. He leaned over and let out a loud breath.

"Oh, Ivan, I'm sorry," she cried. "I didn't mean to actually hit you."

"Don't apologize, Tiff." He laughed. "It's fine, I'll survive." He took a moment, and then stood up to his full height. "See?"

Without thought, she began to rub her hand over his stomach. That simple action generated more of a response than her hitting him. He sucked in his breath and covered her hand with his. Ivan slid her arm up his chest. When it reached his face, he kissed the inside of her wrist.

Suddenly, the air sizzled around them. Without warning, Tiffany used Ivan's weight against him and propelled him to the floor. He pulled her with him, but made sure that she landed on top of him.

She gazed into his eyes. "Are you always prepared for anything?"

"I try to be."

"You need to relax," she instructed. "No more shop talk, no more self-defense lessons. I'm here with you, and I'm fine. You worry too much."

"I'm sorry. It's my job."

"I know. But I'm not work."

He nodded. "You're right. The next time you think I'm being overbearing, just hit me."

She smiled. "Deal."

Ivan kissed Tiffany, and she immediately responded. Moments later, he said, "It's time for me to leave, before I do something...ungentlemanly."

"I don't mind finding out what that is," Tiffany said coyly.

Ivan's eyes smoldered to a golden brown. He got up and helped her to her feet. She immediately jumped in his arms, refusing to let him go.

"Tiff, tell me to leave," he growled into her ear. "Tell me before it's too late, and we both end up sprawled on your bed, and I'm buried inside you."

His sensual words sent shivers up her spine. Her heart beat a steady staccato inside her chest.

"Say it," he commanded.

"I can't," she choked out. "Because I don't want you to leave."

"I don't want to leave, either."

She caressed his jaw. Their eyes met. "Then don't."

It was all the incentive he needed. Ivan swept her into his arms and carried her to the bedroom. He set her down. "It's not too late to reconsider," he told her solemnly.

Tiffany ran her hand up his massive arm. His thick muscles flexed under her firm touch. "Why would I want to do that? I'm not going to change my mind, Ivan. I want you to make love to me."

Ivan leaned her back over his arm and kissed her on the neck. His lips trailed down her chest to the top of her shirt. He kissed her, and then moved lower. When he gently clamped down on her breast through her shirt, Tiffany gasped with pleasure. Her legs grew weak, but Ivan held her in a tight embrace.

"Relax. I've got you, sweetheart. You won't fall," he promised her.

He continued sampling her through the cotton fabric. He used his free hand to ease her top higher. He slid his tongue across her belly, causing her to squirm against him. He picked her up and placed her in the center of the bed. He followed her down. Stretched out next to her, his hand caressed her flat stomach. His fingers moved over the button on her slacks. He unbuttoned them with one flick before he unzipped them. The noise filled the silent room. His hand went lower, and then he palmed her through her pants. Tiffany sucked in her breath.

"How does that feel?" he asked.

"Incredible," she groaned. "Like I'm on fire."

"Are you on fire, Tiff? Are you burning for me, baby?"

She was nodding and saying yes at the same time.

"What do you want me to do next?"

"Touch me—there."

Slowly, Ivan eased his hand down the front of her pants. When he touched her, she was more than ready for him. He teased her flesh with his fingers.

"Ivan." Tiffany writhed on the bed. "Please," she begged.

"Talk to me, sweetheart. Tell me what makes you hot."

"You do," she rasped out.

"Yeah? What about now?" he asked, teasing her with a practiced hand.

"Yes." She raised her hips up off the bed to meet his hand.

Ivan rocked her then—up the precipice, right to the edge and then barreling over the side of it. Tiffany's hands clamped down on his hand to hold it in place. She shook violently against him as he coaxed her to delights that she had only dreamed about. Tiffany called his name repeatedly as tiny electrons fired simultaneously throughout her body. Eventually they subsided, but she was still shaking from the intensity of it.

He kissed her then with infinite tenderness and a promise of more physical delights to come.

"That was incredible," she panted. "You really are an Army of One."

Ivan kissed the bridge of her nose. When she recovered, she pulled him in for a long, lingering kiss.

"I liked that," he said thickly.

"There's much, much more where that came from," Tiffany assured him.

He wore a boyish grin, and he smoothed his hand up her rib cage. "Is that so?"

Before she could answer, Ivan's cell phone rang in his pocket.

"You've got to be kidding me," he complained, before kissing her soundly. "Give me a minute, Tiff."

He eased off her and sat up on the bed to answer his phone. "Mangum," he said tersely.

Tiffany listened with growing disappointment. She sat up. It seemed they would not be finishing what they'd started.

Ivan hung up the phone. "I'm sorry, baby. Something's come up at work that I have to deal with."

"It's okay," she told him. "Go."

He studied her face. "Are you sure, sweetheart?"

She loved when he called her that. It was new, and she liked it. Almost as much as the explosive orgasm he'd just given her. "Yes." She smiled. "I'm sure. I'm just sorry it was before I could…return the favor."

He bent down to kiss her neck. "I'm not going anywhere, Tiffany. I'll be more than happy to take a rain check." He grinned wickedly. "If it's not too late, I'll call you."

"You'd better call me when you get home—no matter what."

"Ah, yes, you take your job seriously."

"You bet I do."

"I'll call you shortly," he promised.

Ivan helped Tiffany off the bed. She zipped her pants back up. Her blouse was still askew, but she didn't bother to fix it. When she turned around, Tiffany gave him a sultry look.

"Are you purposely trying to kill me?" He groaned.

"No, of course not. I need you alive. I'm hardly through with you, Mangum."

She walked him to the door. Tiffany stood on her tiptoes and wrapped her arms around his neck.

"Thanks for coming to my rescue earlier," she whispered. "You saved me a lot of time and headache."

Ivan placed his hand under her chin and tilted her face to meet his. "I'll always come to your rescue." He kissed her a final time and left.

The void Tiffany felt at his departure was instantaneous. It was as though a warm breeze had dissipated, and in its place, nothing but cold air remained. She locked the door and padded into her bedroom to undress. She wanted to be done with her shower when Ivan called her.

Tiffany shuddered. She'd just had the best orgasm of her life. She would be crazed when they finally made love without any interruptions. She didn't know if it would be before or after Ivan returned from Venice, but one thing was clear: Tiffany wanted Ivan with a vengeance, and when they finally came together, it would assuredly be worth waiting for.

Wearing a huge grin, she strolled into the bathroom.

Ivan tried Tiffany again, but got her voice mail. He left a message and hung up. She was probably asleep. He was tired, too. It had been a long day, and thanks to Tiffany tempting his thoughts, it would be an even longer night. He had tasted the pleasures that awaited him, and that preview had only made him want her more. When his cell phone rang, he answered it on the first ring.

"There you are. I thought you'd gone to bed."

"Not without talking to you one last time," she assured him. "I'm glad you're home safe and sound."

"I'm safe, but not sound. I have you to thank for that."

"I know, but now I have something to remember you by," Tiffany purred.

"One night soon, I'll be giving you a lot more to remember me by."

"I wish it were right now."

"So do I. I'm sorry work got in the way."

"It's okay, Ivan. I understand that sometimes work takes precedence."

"Yeah, but I'd prefer it wasn't like that sometimes. You get that, don't you?"

"Of course. You're admirable, dedicated to work, sexy as hell, and now…exasperating."

He chuckled at that. "I'll make it up to you. That's a promise."

They hung up a few minutes later, then Ivan lay on his back with his arms folded behind his head. He was too wired to sleep, but going for a run right now was not on his list of priorities. At the moment, he wanted to remember, in exact detail, every square inch of Tiffany's body that he had probed, kissed, touched and tasted. There was a lot more territory left undiscovered. He hadn't even left on assignment yet, and already he was eagerly anticipating his return.

His cell phone rang ten minutes later. When he saw the number, he grimaced.

"Hi, Debra. It's kind of late to be calling. Are you okay?"

"Hi, Ivan," she replied. "Yes, I'm okay. I wanted you to know that I received your check this month. Thank you."

"You're welcome. Was that all you needed?" he asked when she remained silent. "It's late, and I have to get up early."

"I was hoping we could get together soon and talk?"

"About what?"

"You know, old times. It's been so lonely here since Brian died. I really miss him," she said tearfully.

Ivan sighed. "I know. I'm sorry, Debra, but the next few weeks are going to be hectic for me. I don't think I'll be able to travel up there, but we do need to talk. There's another thing I've been meaning to discuss with you."

"Oh?" she said excitedly. "What is it?"

Ivan decided to just plunge right in. He never liked beating around the bush.

"It's time you evaluated your options, Debra. I know it's been an extremely difficult time for you, and I agreed to help you through this transition period—"

"Yes, you did, and I'm grateful for your financial help, Ivan. I don't know what I would have done without it. You've been kinder to me than I had any right to expect, all things considered. I want you to know how thankful I am for your kindness."

"You're welcome. I'm glad I could help, but when I did, we discussed it being a temporary measure to help get you on your feet. Have you been looking for employment?"

"Yes, of course I have. I have a few possibilities lined up, but it's a slow process. I don't expect to hear anything for a while, but I'm going to keep looking."

"To help with that, Debra, I've asked a local company that we've done business with in the past to give you a call regarding an interview. The job isn't guaranteed, but they are definitely interested in your coming in for an interview. The rest is up to you. You'll have another thirty days of financial support from me, but then it will end. My hope is by then you'll have received good news on the job front and will be starting a new chapter in your life."

There was a long pause before she said, "Thank you, Ivan. Your support has meant the world to me. You don't know how much."

"You're welcome. Be expecting a call early next week. Let me know if you get the job, and good luck."

"I…I'll be sure to do that," she replied. "Good night, Ivan."

Ivan said goodbye and hung up. He set the phone down, and then leaned back against the pillows.

Ivan felt good about setting an end date to his helping Debra. He wanted to sever all ties with her before anything cropped up that would cause problems between him and Tiffany. Her happiness was paramount, and though she said she was okay with the help he was extending to Debra, Ivan was smart enough to know that he didn't want to push his luck. It was his hope that his relationship with Tiffany would continue to progress and move forward.

She represented his future.

Now it was time to bury the past and be done with it.

Chapter 12

"Why do you have such a problem picking out clothes?" Milán posed the question while she lounged on Tiffany's bed.

Tiffany glanced over her shoulder. "You're not helping."

"It's a date to go bowling, not a black-and-white ball."

"I still want to look good," Tiffany said. She held up two outfits and shook them in front of her.

"The one on the right," Milán offered.

"You're wonderful. That was my favorite, too."

"So tell me again what this is about?"

"A few members of Ivan's class are on a bowling team. They invited him to play a game after their practice tonight, and he's invited me to go with him."

"That's cute," Milán replied. "But you don't bowl, do you?"

"Not really," Tiffany said from the bathroom, "but it doesn't matter."

She reappeared wearing a pair of white denim shorts

and the pink Girl Power T-shirt that Ivan had given her. She spun around. "How do I look?"

"Lovely. So are you meeting Ivan there, or is he coming to get you?"

"He's coming here. He always insists on coming to get me. Ask me how long it's been since I had to fill up my gas tank. The man is a perfect gentleman. He comes to get me, drives me wherever we're going, brings me back home and sees me to the door."

"It sounds as if it's getting under your skin a bit."

"It's not that I don't appreciate the gestures, but I can do all these things myself. I was doing all of it before we met."

"Yes, and I recall how much you complained about not being pampered, and having to do it all on your own. You wanted someone to spoil you on occasion and make you feel special—remember?"

"Yes," Tiffany replied with a frown.

"And he's giving you just what you asked for. Why are you resisting it? It's like you're purposely not allowing yourself to be happy, to just enjoy being with a man who's so attentive."

Tiffany flopped into a chair. "Is that what I'm doing?"

Her friend got up and walked over to her. "Honey, this isn't the first time you've mentioned that Ivan being so focused on you is getting under your skin. The question I'm trying to get you to ask yourself is *why* does it bother you so much? You should give that some thought, Tiff. I've got to run. I'm meeting Adrian for dinner." Milán kissed her cheek. "Have fun tonight, and we'll talk later, okay?"

"Thanks," Tiffany said absentmindedly.

She was sitting in the same spot when her doorbell rang minutes later. She stood up and checked her reflection in the mirror, pasted on a big smile and went to answer the door.

* * *

Bowling with Ivan and the group from class was more fun than Tiffany had imagined. She was not good at it, but with Ivan's coaching and the support from her team-mates, she got her first strike five frames into their first game. When they fell, Tiffany screamed with excitement and did a little dance.

"Is that your happy dance?" Ivan laughed.

She spun around a final time before pointing to the scoreboard. "I'm above thirty now," she said triumphantly.

"Way to go," he said supportively. "You're improving."

"Hey, let me take your picture," Gladys said.

Ivan pulled Tiffany to his side while the elderly woman took their picture with her cell phone.

She glanced up at them afterward and said, "I'm taking another one. You two are too boring. Come on, Ivan, get in close and give your woman a smooch!"

He bent down to kiss Tiffany. She wrapped her arms around his waist and leaned into him.

"That's better," Gladys said. "Would you like me to email it to you?"

Ivan's eyes widened. "You know how to do that?"

She rolled her eyes. "Of course I do. My grandkids gave me an iPhone for my birthday, and they've been show-ing me all sorts of stuff. Next week they're teaching me something called "Just Dance." Like I don't know how to dance already."

"Hi." A man came upon the group. "I'm Charles Wa-ters. I work for *ChiTown* magazine." He handed Ivan his card. "Do you have a minute?"

"Sure," Ivan replied.

"I write an online column and get a lot of followers on my social media sites who are interested in commu-nity issues. Colonel Mangum, I heard from a very reliable source that you donate your time and money to help out community-center patrons by teaching self-defense classes and that you've also supported local businesses in our area by installing security systems."

Ivan's eyebrows rose higher. "A reliable source?"

"Yes, sir. I've also heard that your company donates time and money to global and local charities. If you don't mind, I'd like to ask you a few questions and take some pictures?"

Looking decidedly uncomfortable, Ivan seemed about to say no when Tiffany whispered into his hear to remind him of the seniors who were mulling around with excitement.

"They want this for you, Ivan. Just say yes."

"I don't need to draw attention to myself," he whispered, and then smiled at the crowd. "I enjoy what I do," he continued in a subdued voice. "I want to help my community where I can. Nothing more."

"I know," she murmured, "but it's obvious someone must've placed a bug in the reporter's ear. You'll disappoint them if you say no."

He glanced around for a moment, and then said yes. A round of cheers went up, and the group buzzed around the table where Ivan was being interviewed.

Charles took a few minutes to ask Ivan and Tiffany some questions, then he turned to a few members of the Ivan's class before following up with a few digital pictures.

"I'll have these up in a few days, and I'll email you both the link to the magazine and my social media sites."

"Great," Ivan replied. "I'll have my community-outreach team add them to my company's website, as well."

"Thanks again," Charles said. Suddenly he leaned forward. "I'm not supposed to tell, but my grandmother is friends with one of your students, and she insisted that I interview you. She couldn't sing your praises enough, and now I can see why. What you both do is important to our seniors and our community."

"It's our pleasure," Ivan said sincerely.

"Yes, it is. I know I've enjoyed being Ivan's assistant. It's a great feeling to empower others to have confidence in their abilities and feel safe," Tiffany added.

He shook Ivan's and Tiffany's hands and then left.

"That was fun," she said to Ivan.

"It actually was," he admitted. He leaned in and kissed her. "Thanks for insisting I do the interview. I was surprised how much fun it was, and you're right, our group really did enjoy it."

"Oh, yeah? I think I'm ready to bring the pain, Mangum."

A loud rumble echoed around their lane as everyone resumed their bowling match.

"What happened to bringing the pain?" he asked Tiffany that night on the phone. "I've just loaded up the pictures so now all our friends will know how bad I kicked your heinie in bowling."

"Hey, I broke seventy so I'm happy."

"That's true, you did. The only person who did worse than you was the guy who had a cast on, and he wasn't even playing."

Tiffany gasped. "Hey, I was kicking butt and you know it. I won for best improved, didn't I?"

"That's because everyone felt sorry for you."

"That may be true," she said with a chuckle. "I had a great time tonight, Ivan. Thanks for taking me."

"You're welcome, and it was my pleasure. It's been a long time since I've gotten out and just enjoyed myself like that. It was nice."

"I agree. It's so easy to get caught up in the day-to-day that you forget to go out and just enjoy yourself sometimes. You know, throw caution to the wind and just act silly and not care who sees you, or what other people think."

"Well, I'd say we did that in spades tonight," Ivan added.

"Yes, we did."

"I'm looking forward to our date."

Tiffany smiled. "Me, too."

They spoke on the phone a few more minutes, and then said goodbye.

After Ivan hung up, he glanced at his cell phone. He had loaded their pictures on his social networking sites, and he checked out the comments. He smiled. He felt incredibly happy when they were out together, and he always looked forward to seeing her. He was truly dreading his business trip, but he had decided to get Tiffany something beautiful for her birthday while he was gone.

He had not thought about what he would do for her yet, but he knew it would be special.

His last thoughts before drifting off to sleep were of Tiffany—what he was going to get her for her birthday, and what he planned on doing with the leftover icing.

How was she going to survive a week without Ivan? Tiffany asked herself this question a dozen times.

He had lit a fire in her over the past few days, and it wasn't about to be extinguished by some sexy promises made during their late-night conversations. She wanted all of him, and this time nothing short of them consummating their feelings would do.

Just then Tiffany's cell phone rang. She picked it up and looked at the screen. Blocked. Normally those types of calls meant an annoying telemarketer, or someone trying not to be traced. "Hello?"

There was a stretch of silence, followed by a loud click in her ear.

"Strange," she said into the phone before hanging up.

Tiffany made it till about four o'clock before she told Celeste that she was heading home. As she drove, she noticed storm clouds moving in. It was sunny for the moment, so she put her windows down and cranked up the music. While she was jamming, her Bluetooth kicked in and she heard her phone ringing. She turned the music down and answered.

"Hello?"

"Hey, honey."

"Hi, Ms. Jeannie. How are you?"

"Running around like a fox in a henhouse. I've got so many things to wrap up before Saturday."

"Anything I can help you with?"

"No, dear, I've got my family on party detail. They aren't happy, but they'll get over it."

"I'll be there early on Saturday to help out," Tiffany assured her.

"Ivan called to tell me that he won't be able to make it. He said he's got to go out of town, but then you knew that, didn't you?"

Warning bells were clamoring in Tiffany's head. She had to tread carefully. "Yes, he did mention it the last time I saw him."

Just recalling their last encounter had her fidgeting in her seat.

"Cliff, it doesn't go there," Norma Jean yelled. "I'm sorry. I've got to run dear, before my husband breaks something. I'll see you on Saturday. And be early. I've got some great things lined up."

"Will do," she promised before ending the call.

Tiffany wondered if Norma Jean suspected anything. She brushed that fear aside. One thing was certain—Jeannie did not do subtle. It wasn't in her nature.

When Tiffany got home, she sprang into action. She wanted to look her best for Ivan's last night in town. She chose a sensual, floral body lotion and a dress guaranteed to drive him crazy.

A while ago she had purchased a silky, violet-blue, spaghetti-strap dress with a diamond-shaped cutout in the middle of her back. It exposed a fair amount of skin without being too overwhelming. Tiffany felt it was the perfect night to christen it. She picked a pair of silver, jewel-studded sandals to go with it. For her hair, she chose a softer, sleek look and shimmering violet-tinted lip gloss. She was putting on her silver teardrop earrings when the doorbell rang. She glanced at the clock on her nightstand. It was seven o'clock on the dot. Excitement fluttered within her. "Right on time," she said aloud.

When she opened the door, Ivan's eyes devoured her. His stunned expression was all the validation she needed. She felt like a knockout.

"Wow."

Ivan scanned her entire body again before he spoke. "You're stunning. I feel like it's my birthday—and you're my gift."

She beamed. "You haven't seen the full view." She turned around to show him the back, and felt ultra sexy when he whistled appreciatively.

"You're wearing the hell out of that dress, Miss Gentry."

"Thank you, Colonel Mangum."

While Ivan drove, they discussed the details of his trip.

"I'll print out a copy of my itinerary for you," he told her. "Right now, it's looking like I'll just be gone a week."

"You think that'll change?"

"It might, depending on my client's schedule. I'm at his disposal."

She nodded. "Ms. Jeannie called me earlier. She wasn't thrilled you aren't coming, but I told her I'd get there early to help out." Tiffany stared out the window. "Ivan, where do you live?" She laughed. "You've been driving almost thirty minutes. I don't know why, but I just assumed you lived closer to downtown."

"My parents' house is in Beverly. I had an apartment in

town, but I gave it up when I decided to spend the summer helping Cole renovate some stuff in the house and keep an eye on GiGi," he told her.

A few minutes later, they pulled into the circular driveway and he shut off the engine. "We're here."

Tiffany's mouth dropped open. "*This* is your home?"

He walked around and opened her door to help her out.

She stared up the stone steps. From there she saw a landing of large slate tiles, and on it a pair of black wrought-iron chairs with a small table between them.

Tiffany turned to him. "It's a mini stone castle," she exclaimed, glancing around the heavily wooded lot. "I didn't know they had hills in Chicago. Ivan, this place is gorgeous. How big is this thing, anyway?"

Ivan slipped her hand in his and guided her toward the stairs. "Only seven thousand square feet."

"Only? My loft could fit into this thing several times. You must feel claustrophobic coming to my house."

"Not really." He kissed her. "Actually, I'm quite content in it, especially in your fourteen-by-twenty-square-foot bedroom."

She smiled. "You're ridiculous."

He unlocked the front door, and they went in. "Welcome to Mangum Manor," he said in his best Count Dracula voice. "Come on, I'll give you a tour."

The house had arched doorways, and they all led off the main foyer. A living room was on the left with six windows on each side of the room that let in loads of natural light. The fireplace had a five-pillar wrought-iron holder with cream-colored candles. The floor was hardwood, and there were wood beams spaced across the high ceilings. The furniture was neutral, and there was a large colorful area rug, plus paintings and accessories that introduced color into the room.

Tiffany went across the hall into the dining room. The

huge wood table and chairs looked like they were from another century. Down the hall, she saw a circular room with windows surrounding it on three sides, low bookshelves and an oval table and decorative rug in the middle of the room.

"The library, I presume?"

"Yep. This is where Cole and I did most of our homework."

The family room had a huge flat-panel screen on the wall with another fireplace and leather furniture. It was homey, and Tiffany could imagine many a family gathering spent there. She picked up one of the pictures sitting on a table. It was a family portrait. Ivan and Cole's mother was a well-tanned woman with strawberry-blond hair and the same amber eyes that Ivan had. Their father was tall, with a mocha-brown complexion and kind brown eyes. He exuded confidence and strength, just like Ivan. They were a good-looking family.

She set the portrait down. A lump formed in her throat. Her parents' home also had a myriad of family portraits, all of them filled with smiles. From the outside looking in, her family appeared happy and her parents in love.

"All an illusion," she whispered.

"What?"

Startled, she turned to Ivan, forcing the shadows away.

"Hey, what's the matter?"

"Nothing. I'm fine."

Ivan placed a hand at her chin and titled her face up to meet his. "If you're fine, why did you look so sad a moment ago?"

Did anything get past him? Tiffany tried again. "No reason. You have a lovely family, Ivan."

Ivan observed her momentarily before he said, "Wait till you meet them. Especially my grandmother—but I have to warn you. She has no filter. You don't know what she'll say at any given moment."

"She sounds like another matriarch we know."

"That's probably why I like Norma Jean so much," Ivan concluded.

Tiffany encouraged him to continue the tour. He showed her the galley-style kitchen. While the other rooms held a hint of old European tradition, the kitchen was ultramodern—it had granite countertops, stainless-steel commercial-grade appliances and all the latest kitchen gadgets. Ivan showed her the half bath that he and his brother had been working on.

"The basement has a guest suite, laundry and exercise rooms, and another full bath. We'll skip that and go upstairs."

Tiffany peeked into a small office right off the second-floor landing, and then saw his parents' master suite and Cole's room. Each room had a bathroom en suite.

Ivan's bedroom was pale gray with a white tray ceiling. His furniture was black and his bedding bright white, with a rich gray comforter and decorative pillows sprawled across it. He had a sitting area and an amazing view of the well-manicured backyard and stone patio.

"This suits you perfectly," she replied, looking around his room.

"Thank you, but I can't take all the credit. My mother redesigned it while I was out of the country. Personally, I think she did it on purpose," he added. "Come on, Cole wants to say hello before he leaves."

"He won't be here?"

Ivan shook his head. "He's got a date, and I doubt he'll be back till some ungodly hour in the morning."

"You don't say?" She grinned.

He wrapped his arms around her and kissed her. "Have

I told you how sexy you look in that damned backless dress?"

"It's not backless," she protested. "It's just a little revealing."

"I'd love to reveal a lot more," he ground out. "Let's go before I forget I have a brother."

They found Cole in the basement working out.

"Good to see you again, Tiffany. I'd hug you, but I'm way too sweaty."

"No worries, I'll get two next time," Tiffany told him.

Cole turned to Ivan. "Has she met GiGi?"

"Not yet."

Tiffany spun around. "Why?"

"Cut it out," Ivan said. "You're going to make Tiffany nervous."

A wicked smile etched Cole's face. "So, what dirt would you like me to dish about my big brother?"

"Hmm…is he always so serious? Or does he cut loose when nobody's looking?"

"Are you kidding? Ivan wouldn't know how to relax if it came in a bottle and was approved by the FDA."

"I relax plenty," he protested.

"Uh-huh. Unconscious relaxing doesn't count, big brother."

"Don't mind chatterbox here." He wrapped an arm around her. "Come on, I've got a great dinner that'll be ready in fifteen minutes."

Ivan glared at his brother from behind Tiffany's back, but Cole just waved.

When they reached the kitchen, Tiffany looked at the stove top, then at Ivan.

"I thought you said dinner would be ready in fifteen minutes? I didn't smell anything when we came in. Is it in the oven, or do we need to warm something up?"

"Nope."

Just then the doorbell rang. Ivan winked. "Dinner's ready."

Tiffany couldn't contain her laughter. "Well, in that case, let's eat."

When he returned, he carried several large bags. He set them on the counter and then retrieved dinnerware, place settings and glasses.

"Would you like to eat inside, or on the patio?"

"It doesn't look like we're getting rain after all, so I vote for outside."

He headed for the door. "Whatever my lady wants, she gets."

They both made two trips carrying what was needed for their meal. Tiffany arranged the table while Ivan brought out the wine bottle he'd chilled, and glasses. Tiffany arranged the food on their plates, and Ivan lit candles and turned on the stereo system. Soft music drifted through the outdoor speakers. By the time it was done, the sunlight was waning.

They both sat down and admired their handiwork.

"I think we work well together," she said proudly.

"The last time we were together was proof of that."

She blushed, remembering their interrupted lovemaking session. "I thought it was, too."

They made a toast and began eating.

"This is delicious," she said after taking a bite of food. "Where did you get it?"

"My parents are friends with a local chef. I asked him to provide something spectacular."

Tiffany stared down at her roasted rack of lamb with a red-wine reduction sauce, asparagus and herb-roasted baby potatoes. "I'd say he knocked it out of the park."

While they were eating, Cole stuck his head out the patio door.

"A driver from Nigel's just dropped off your dessert. I'm gone. Good seeing you, Tiffany. Don't be a stranger."

"Thanks, Cole." She turned to Ivan. "I don't plan to be."

Chapter 13

"Do you always do things on such a grand scale?"

Ivan grinned. "Only when I'm...motivated." He took her hand and spun her around so that her back was toward him. "What about you? This dress is making a heck of a statement, too."

Tiffany turned back around. "I was...motivated."

After dinner they cleaned up and put the leftovers away. They camped out on the couch and watched a movie. Halfway through, Ivan said, "Would you like your dessert now?"

"Definitely."

She sat up, but he stopped her.

"I'll get it, you relax."

"If I relax any more, I'll be asleep. You sit, and I'll go. That's an order," she added for good measure.

He looked surprised. "Yes, ma'am."

Tiffany returned with a tray holding two small plates

and two glasses of milk. She set it on the table and handed him a plate and fork.

"I see you found everything okay."

"I'm very good at foraging."

Ivan chuckled. "Thank you. How'd you know I like milk with my cake?"

"Just a calculated guess." She took a bite of the fruit torte, and then closed her eyes to savor the taste.

"Good call," he told her after sampling his dessert.

"You, too. This cake is delicious."

When they were done, Tiffany stretched out against him. It felt good to have his arm draped around her shoulders. It reminded her that she missed having this connection with a man. It wasn't long before she fell asleep.

"Hey," Ivan whispered into her ear some time later. "Wake up, sleepyhead. Movie's over."

"It is?" she said groggily. "Darn, I was looking forward to the end."

"Don't worry, I recorded it for you."

Ivan got up and helped her to her feet. Without any shoes on, Tiffany came to his chest. She tilted her head back.

"This has been such a great evening, Ivan. It's hard to believe that this time tomorrow, you'll be gone."

"I'll be back before you know it."

Tiffany wrapped her arms around the wide expanse of his chest and rested her face against him. She could feel his heart beating against her temple. "You'll be gone…I'll definitely know it."

Tiffany thought about the brief time they had known each other. It had been over a month now, but it felt much longer. "Ivan, I don't want this night to end."

His touched the side of her face. "It doesn't have to. Stay with me."

She gazed up at him. He was so appealing to her.

"Hey," he said when she didn't answer. "You can sleep

in the guest room if you'd prefer not to sleep in my bed. There's no pressure, Tiff. I'm fine with whatever you decide. I just want you here with me."

"I know you'd never pressure me. I want to spend as much time as I can with you before you go."

He picked her up so that she was eye level with him. "Yeah?"

"Yes. And I'm not sleeping in the guest room," she clarified. "Unless that's where you'll be."

He set her on her feet. Ivan reached up and tilted her head to the side to kiss the pulse at her neck. Tiffany leaned into the embrace. "Are you ready to go up?"

Tiffany knew there was a lot more entwined in that question than mere sleeping arrangements. He was asking her to make love to him. "Yes," she told him. "I'm definitely ready."

He turned the television off and left the dishes right where they were.

When they reached the base of the stairs, he picked her up. She let out a gasp. Ivan ran up the stairs with her like he did it every day. When he got to his room, he went in and kicked the door shut with his foot, then set her down.

"You're so beautiful."

She beamed at his compliment. "I've got a confession to make."

His eyebrows rose higher. "Do tell."

"When I first saw you, I had to remind myself to breathe."

With a steady hand, Ivan touched the silky outline of her hip and then moved around to follow the shape of her rear end. His fingers inched higher to trace the cutout at the back of her dress before slipping around to the front to sketch her right breast. His eyes never left her face. "I know the feeling."

Tiffany quivered from the emotions his touch evoked.

She felt like her body jolted awake under his ministrations. It felt as if she had been asleep all her adult life, and only now, with Ivan, had she begun to blossom. It was intoxicating. He was intoxicating.

She ran a hand up his shirt to the open area at the top. She caressed his chest before undoing the buttons one by one. When she finished, Tiffany slid the shirt off of him. It landed in a heap behind him.

"My turn."

She allowed her hands to roam over the broad expanse of his chest. She was as thorough as he was in his study. Ivan remained completely still while she explored him.

Tiffany noticed several scars that ran along his ribs, stomach and left pectoral. Tiffany solemnly traced them with her fingers, and then bent down to kiss each one.

Ivan released a harsh breath. "God, Tiff."

"You like that?" she asked, tickling him with her tongue.

There was a clap of thunder that sounded outside his bedroom window.

She moved her lips lower, teasing his stomach, and then the skin below his navel as she went. She unzipped his pants and then licked a path downward, blowing warm trails of air as she went. With steady hands, Tiffany eased his pants down his large, muscled legs. When they hit the floor, he stepped out of them.

She touched him through the cotton boxer briefs he was wearing, reveling in the feel of his warm, firm flesh. When she stroked him, a low moan escaped his lips.

"What do you want me to do next?" she whispered.

A boom broke through the silence and shook the windows.

"Looks like a storm's coming," she breathed against his stomach.

"It won't come close to matching the one in here," he replied in a firm voice.

Now it was Ivan's turn to explore. He knelt down and grasped the hem of her dress. As he raised it higher, his fingers grazed her skin along the way. He caressed Tiffany's ankles, knees, thighs, waist and then her upper torso.

"As delectable as this looks, I'd prefer to see what's underneath it."

He eased the dress up over her head and then moved to put it on a chair. Tiffany shook her head and took it from him. She dropped it on the floor next to his shirt.

"I don't want you going anywhere," she said boldly.

Ivan stepped back to take in the entire picture of her wearing black thong panties and nothing else.

"Do you know how sexy you are?"

She took a good look at him. It was there in his eyes. In the controlled strength he held at bay like a panther waiting to strike. Finally, Tiffany could *see* how much he desired her. He held nothing back. It was as potent a feeling as if she had been injected with an aphrodisiac.

Tiffany gazed into his eyes. "You just told me."

Suddenly, he gripped her shoulders and pulled her in to kiss him in one motion.

"I'm trying to remain a gentleman, but it's getting harder by the minute. All I want to do is ravage you."

She bit his lower lip before slipping her hand inside the waistband of his briefs. "I think I'd prefer your not-so-gentlemanly side right about now."

Ivan was having a hell of a time concentrating on anything except how good Tiffany's lips felt on his body, and the havoc her fingers worked on his manhood. It had been his intention to hold off until he returned from Italy before making Tiffany his. That had been the goal, but even with rigorous discipline, military background and good intentions, Ivan was not strong enough to stop now. He heard rain pelting the windows and another loud clap of thunder, but unless a tornado was imminent, he wasn't going to worry about it. Right now his little vixen was driving him crazy, and he was going to make the most of it.

With a Herculean effort, he stayed her hand.

"What's the matter?"

"Nothing, sweetheart. I couldn't be happier, believe me, but there are other things I've been aching to do."

Ivan picked her up and placed her in the center of his king-size bed. There was no greater picture than Tiffany splayed across his bed, almost naked, and waiting for him with a look of complete trust and desire.

"You have too many clothes on," he said thickly.

Tiffany eyed him brazenly. "So do you."

Ivan stripped out of his boxer briefs and knelt on the bed in front of her. He took his time sliding her panties down over her hips, and then her legs. He threw them behind him with great flourish. Tiffany giggled. Her laughter faded when Ivan reached up to stroke her fully. "You don't know how much I've wanted to pick up where we left off."

Ivan made good on his promise of learning what drove Tiffany wild. He took his time discovering the many nuances of her body. After exploring and touching her in various places, he cued in to her sensitive spots and gave them his complete attention. It wasn't long before Tiffany sat up on her elbows.

"Ivan, I can't wait anymore. I want you inside me now."

He retrieved a condom out of his nightstand drawer, and after putting it on, he settled over her.

"Relax, sweetheart. You're tense."

"Am I? Sorry. The anticipation is driving me crazy."

"I know the feeling. I just don't want to hurt you."

Tiffany took a few deep breaths when she felt him easing inside her.

"Are you okay?" he asked in a strained voice.

"I'm fine," she assured him.

When Ivan pushed forward, Tiffany sucked in her breath. She felt like smiling in pure satisfaction as she felt her muscles give way to accommodate his size. With purposeful strides, he set the pace and she held on to his shoulders to catch the rhythm. For Tiffany, there were no words to describe what it felt like to finally be making love with Ivan. No daydreams or fantasies could ever match the real thing. He coaxed her body to reach heights it never had before.

A harmonious concert played out between her body, mind and heart, and for Tiffany, it was epic. Whatever she could reach, she explored. When she stuck her tongue in his ear, he almost came off the bed.

"Baby, you do that again, and this roller coaster will be over before we get to the first loopty-loop."

She burst out laughing. "Sorry."

"Don't apologize, it felt good—just a little too good."

Later, Ivan tensed, and then he cursed.

Tiffany wasn't close yet, but she found out seconds later that with Ivan, her not climaxing wasn't an option. He rolled her over so that she was on top. She steadied herself by placing her hands on his chest. He held her waist and set a faster tempo. Her body reacted instantly.

"Ivan," she gasped.

He leaned up and held her tight. Tiffany locked her legs around his waist.

"Time to let go, sweetheart."

His gentle command was enough for her to do just that. Tiffany became engulfed in a sea so sweet, she never wanted it to end. A few seconds later, Ivan buried his face against her neck and let himself get caught up in the wave, too.

They stilled moments later before collapsing against the sheets. Outside, another clap of thunder sounded overhead.

A few minutes later, Ivan ran a hand over Tiffany's backside.

"Are you alive?"

She murmured into his neck. "Mmm-hmm. You?"

"Sort of," he replied. Ivan sat up and swung his legs over the side of the bed. Tiffany protested the lack of warmth.

"Where are you going?"

"To the bathroom. Come on," he said. "Let's take a shower."

Tiffany dragged herself up, and he helped her off the bed. "Okay, but then I'm getting back in this bed, and I'm going to sleep for ten hours."

"That's a deal," he promised her.

Ivan turned on the shower and adjusted the temperature. He got in first before helping her into the hot spray. Ivan had a rain showerhead that cascaded water over them.

"I've never used one of these before," she told him, and instantly perked up. "This is neat."

"Glad you like it. Now come here."

Ivan washed Tiffany's back. She returned the favor when he was done, and then they washed each other. They got out and towel-dried off before returning to bed.

They were entwined in each other's arms a while before Tiffany said, "Ivan?"

"Yeah, sweetheart."

"Did I hear thunder earlier?"

He chuckled. "Yes, you did. It stormed earlier."

She yawned. "Hmm…I didn't notice."

"Then my mission is complete," Ivan teased.

"So is mine," she said sleepily.

"Really? What mission was that?"

"Operation Seduction…did it work?"

His chest shook with mirth. He kissed her shoulder. "I'd say you nailed it, babe."

* * *

Tiffany awoke slightly disoriented. It was still dark outside. After a moment, she remembered where she was. *Ivan's house.* She turned over and reached for him. Her hand connected with air. "Ivan?" she called out.

"Hey," she heard him say from across the room.

She sat up. "Hi. What are you doing?"

"I wasn't sleepy, so I figured I'd read over my prep work for the new client."

Tiffany yawned. She had slept well curled up next to him in his massive bed. A clap of thunder sounded outside, followed by the sound of heavy rain. "What time is it?"

"Zero two hundred."

"Oh. Are you finished?"

"I can be."

"Good. Can you come back to bed?"

Ivan set his work down, and then sauntered over to the bed and climbed in. He gathered Tiffany up in his arms. "Hey, beautiful. I didn't wake you, did I?"

"No," she said. "Not exactly."

"What does that mean?"

"That you didn't wake me per se, but you did in my dream—it was pretty hot."

"Is that so?" Ivan rolled Tiffany under him. He kissed her neck and grinned down at her with purpose in his eyes. "Let's see if I can give that dream of yours some competition."

This time, when Tiffany awoke hours later, Ivan wasn't in the room. She stretched languorously. His bed was extremely comfortable, and between it and his massive body, and being spent from lovemaking, she had slept like the dead. Reluctantly, Tiffany got up. A pile of clothes and a note were at the end of the bed. She opened it and saw

Ivan's bold handwriting and three words on the page. *In the kitchen*.

In the bathroom, she stared in the mirror at her reflection. Aside from having tousled hair, a sheet mark across her right cheek and a huge grin, she looked no different. *I sure feel different*. Her body hummed with newfound energy.

Ivan had set out towels and a basket of bath products. Excited, she glanced over the mesh sponge, shower gel, body lotion and deodorant. No guy she had ever known was that thoughtful. Clearly Ivan was used to planning for every contingency.

She finished her morning routine, got dressed and went downstairs.

When he saw her, he strode over and kissed her soundly. "Good morning," he whispered into her ear. "How'd you sleep?"

"When I did get some sleep," she said, "it was great."

With a devilish grin, Ivan picked her up in his arms. "I'm absolutely not apologizing for keeping you…busy last night."

She wrapped her legs around his waist. "You'd better not," she warned. "Last night was…" She blushed just thinking about it.

Ivan kissed her tenderly. "That about sums it up for me, too." He set her down. "It's incredible how you make my T-shirt and shorts look erotic."

"I'll bet," she told him. "I had to double knot the shorts, and I'm swimming in this shirt."

"Yeah, but you still look hot."

The way he said it, combined with the heated look he gave her, made her quiver. "Why did you let me sleep so late? I could've helped with breakfast."

"I'm used to getting up early, and I wanted you to get some rest. After all, you had a long night."

"We had a long night," she corrected. "Then she took a container of orange juice and two glasses into the dining room. Ivan followed with a platter of banana pancakes, sausage, bacon, scrambled eggs and a bowl of fresh fruit. He set them in front of her before he sat down.

She looked at him. "And who's supposed to eat all this? It looks like you cooked for a small village."

"I forgot Cole wasn't here this morning. Between the two of us, there's usually nothing left."

"It's like a buffet." Tiffany fixed her plate, and then one with more generous portions for Ivan.

"I hope you don't mind, but I opened the basket of fancy toiletries in the bathroom."

"You were supposed to. I left them for you."

Suddenly, a thought popped into Tiffany's head. She glanced up. "Do you always keep that in your bathroom? You know, just in case?"

"Just in case what?"

"You know…if you ever need it."

Ivan choked on the pancakes he was eating. "Are you trying to ask me if I keep all that girlie stuff around for women spending the night?"

She bristled when he burst out laughing.

Tiffany pushed her chair back and got up. She went to stride past him, but he caught her and plopped her into his lap.

"Let go."

She sat there stiffly in his arms, not moving an inch. "I mean it, Ivan. Let go."

"Not until you tell me why you think I have women parading in and out of my parents' home so frequently that I'd need to keep a supply of women's toiletries."

"How about you answer my question first?"

Ivan searched her face. "Are you really angry?" he asked, suddenly serious.

He released her immediately. Tiffany got up and took her plate to the kitchen without answering him. She threw the remainder of her breakfast away and rinsed her plate and glass. She was about to put them in the dishwasher when Ivan's hand reached out to stop her.

"Tiffany, we need to talk about this."

"I don't want to talk."

"I can see that, but do you really want to spend my last day in town angry?"

With a loud sigh, Tiffany set down the plate and shut off the water. She spun around to face him. "No."

Instead of attempting to hold her, Ivan moved back and leaned against the counter across from her.

"When have I ever given you the impression that I have a revolving bedroom door? I meant what I said about working all the time, and living a monklike existence. Did you think that was just a ploy to get you into bed?"

"No," she admitted.

"Then why would you automatically think I was trying to play you?"

Tiffany was at a loss for words. It was obvious that her accusations irritated him, but once she went down the road of self-doubt, it was impossible to veer off the path. How could she tell him what had been going on in her mind when she didn't even understand it? One minute she was fine, and the next she was imaging all sorts of things involving Ivan and other women.

"I wasn't… Okay, maybe I was…just a little," she admitted.

Ivan tilted his head to the side.

"Fine, I was a lot jealous. I don't know what came over me. It popped into my head just now, and I started wondering what guy is thoughtful enough to keep those kinds of things around for a woman? I didn't come up with any."

He took a deep breath. "My mother is big on making

sure that any overnight guests feel at home. She's the one who brought the basket of toiletries. It was unopened, remember? She also keeps toothpaste, toothbrushes, shampoo and a boatload of other stuff she thinks people might forget. She's got a whole section in the linen closet of stuff like this."

"Ivan, I'm sorry I acted like that. It was completely uncalled for. I just… Last night was perfect, and just thinking about you with someone else…really didn't sit well with me."

Ivan pushed off the counter and took her hands in his. He kissed them one at a time. "It's just you, Tiff. Got it?"

Unable to help the megawatt smile that illuminated her face, she nodded. A tear slid down her cheek. He brushed it away with his thumb and wrapped his arms around her.

"And I thought last night was perfect, too. I didn't have time to arrange fireworks, but we did have thunder and lightning," he joked.

"Thank you," she murmured. "I needed to hear that."

"You're welcome."

He gazed down at her. "We survived our first disagreement."

Tiffany buried her head against his chest. "If it wasn't for me, we wouldn't have had it to begin with."

"Tiffany, we're going to argue sometimes. It's not uncommon."

"I know that better than most," she said drily.

Ivan tilted her head up to look into her eyes. "Yes, I guess that's true. You've definitely heard your fair share of arguments from what you've told me about your home life, but you can't let it consume you and dictate your actions now."

She grimaced. "How do you mean?"

"We can't always get along, sweetheart, and I don't think

you want us walking on pins and needles for fear of making the other one angry, do you?"

She shook her head. "No, that's not realistic."

"No, it's not. But I will promise you something."

"What?"

"I'll always, always want to have makeup sex."

"I'm glad because I will, too."

He picked her up and headed out of the kitchen.

"What are you doing?" she shrieked.

"Well, we've had our first fight. Now it's time to get to the lovin'."

Chapter 14

Now, that was definitely something to remember him by! Tiffany was curled up on the family-room couch thinking about the "makeup sex" they'd just shared. They hadn't even made it to the bed. It was quick, explosive and her body still hummed from the aftermath like a well-tuned engine.

Ivan sat down on the couch next to her. "I don't have to ask what's got you smiling like that."

"Nope." Tiffany sat up and kissed him.

"I forgot to mention that I don't normally have the ringer on my personal phone when I'm on duty, so if you need to reach me and I don't answer, text me and I'll get back to you as soon as I can. I wrote down my assistant Curtis's direct number on the itinerary. He can get a message to me if it's an emergency."

She sat up. "Okay."

Suddenly, she felt overwhelmed with emotion. It dawned on Tiffany how much she would miss him, especially now.

There was a higher level of intimacy between them, and with it a new sense of awareness that Tiffany didn't have before. Her need for him was heightened, which made her wonder if it would have been better to wait until he came home from Italy before they made love. Well, it was a moot point now. They had—a lot—it was incredible, and for Tiffany it was going to be a long week.

By the time Cole returned home, they had just finished lunch. He said hello and went straight to the fridge for a bottle that had a green concoction in it. Ivan sauntered over to the cabinet, pulled out a large bottle of Advil and handed it to his brother.

He grunted his thanks and then surveyed the couple. "How was your evening, or do I need to ask?"

The high-wattage smile from Tiffany may have been proof enough, but she added, "I think it was pretty spectacular, don't you, Ivan? I mean, we barely got the last of the furniture reglued before you got here. Good thing Ivan will be away for a week so that it can dry. Unfortunately, one of the goose-down pillows didn't make it."

Ivan roared with laughter. He observed his brother. "I think you'd better think twice before trying to put Tiffany on the spot."

Cole laughed, too, and took another sip of his drink. "Evidently, our Tiffany is no shrinking violet. That's cool. I like a challenge."

"You'd better go to bed, little brother. You look like warmed-over crap. If you get hungry later, there're leftovers in the fridge. I've got an assignment, but I'll call and check in with you later."

Cole nodded and gingerly lowered his head to the table.

Ivan glanced at Tiffany. "And that's why I don't drink anything stronger than beer."

"Hope you feel better, Cole," she whispered, before following Ivan back upstairs.

"How about we take you home so that you can change your clothes? I'll stay as long as I can and leave for the airport from your house. That way we can spend more time together."

"I like the way you think, Colonel Mangum."

Ivan gave her a small bag to carry her dress in. She placed the basket of toiletries he gave her into his linen closet to save for next time.

"I'll call you tonight and you can tell me how the party went," he said as he packed.

"Ha. Don't worry, if things get really interesting, I'll send a video," she promised.

Later, they were in the middle of shopping when Tiffany's cell phone rang. She retrieved it from her purse and answered it.

"Hello?" She glanced at the screen. It was another blocked call. Tiffany hung up and shoved the phone back into her bag.

"Wrong number?"

"I have no idea. It was a blocked call. I've had several lately."

Ivan stopped walking. "Does the person say anything?"

"No. I've had a few voice-mail messages, but nobody says anything, and after a while they just hang up."

He frowned. "When did this start?"

"I don't know. Last week, I guess."

"Why didn't you tell me?"

She shrugged. "It didn't cross my mind."

His jaw clenched. He set the produce that he had picked up back in the basket and guided her to a more secluded area.

"What's the matter?" she asked once they were alone.

"Someone is playing on your phone, and it didn't cross your mind to mention it?" he said.

"Honestly, no."

Ivan shook his head. "The next time it happens, I want to know."

"Why? It's not like you can do anything about it." She stared at him. "Why are you getting upset about this? It's just a phone call."

"How would you know? It never crossed your mind for a second that it could be more than that? Not everyone around you is harmless, Tiffany. You're a single woman living alone in a busy city. You need to be concerned about a person who doesn't want you knowing their identity calling you repeatedly and hanging up."

"Well, you're the security expert," she snapped. "What would you have done?"

Ivan retrieved his cell phone from his pocket and dialed a number. "Mike, I need a favor."

He relayed Tiffany's cell number to his friend, and instructed him to call him later with a report. He ended the call and shoved his phone back into his pocket.

"When I find out who's been calling your phone and harassing you, I'll let you know."

He stalked off, leaving her alone. Tiffany stood there and waited. Finally, Ivan turned around, let out a harsh breath and walked back over to where she was standing. "I'm sorry for losing my temper," he said in a quieter voice. "It's just that I've seen a great deal of bad in the world, Tiffany. I've also seen what happens to women and girls who are misfortunate enough to be on the receiving end of a man's anger, lust or both, and be powerless to defend themselves. I...I don't want that to be you." He struggled to maintain his composure. "And when you're dismissive about the possibility that you could find yourself in a situation that you can't get out of—"

"I get it," she said quietly. "I'm sorry, Ivan. I forget sometimes that you've seen a world that I know exists, but that

I've never seen, and probably never will. I shouldn't have gotten snarky with you about it. If anything, I should've been more receptive to your concern. I just got angry at you thinking that I couldn't take care of myself. I realize now that in certain situations, that may be true."

"When have I ever said that you can't take care of yourself?"

"Maybe not verbally, but your actions say it loud and clear."

A confused expression crossed his face.

"You check my apartment every time you bring me home."

"And you think that translates to me thinking you can't take care of yourself?"

"Sometimes, yes. I've had to fend for myself a lot. Well, it was more by choice. I saw how much my mother relied on my father to do things for her. He made all the decisions in our household. Though my mother worked, she deferred to him in all things. I didn't pay it any attention because we were fine. But when they began having problems and it grew worse, and he left, that's when I saw it."

"Saw what?"

"How…incapacitated she was. My mother wasn't able to regain her sense of self after they broke up. She was so wrapped up in him that she couldn't seem to function on her own. And the more time passed, the more bitter she became. In public she was fine—she went to work, came home and went places with the rest of the family. But at home it was…different. It was like a part of her was missing, and she didn't care what happened to her. It broke my heart, Ivan," Tiffany said. "I was her daughter, and yet nothing I did made her feel better. That's when I knew I would be different."

"Different how?"

"I refused to make the same mistakes my mother made. I would always provide for myself. Even when I fell in love, I swore I'd make sure that if anything happened, I would be okay."

He ran a hand over his face. It was a few moments before he answered. "Tiffany, I know you can take care of yourself. Your independence is one of the things I admire about you. I like that fact that you have your own business, and if situations arise, you can handle yourself. If I made you feel like I was trying to take that away from you, I apologize. It was never my intention. It's just what I'm used to doing. My father instilled into us from a young age that we should always take care of a woman. Though Cole may seem like he forgets at times, we're used to being gentlemen. Holding doors, paying for meals, ensuring that a woman is provided for… It's second nature, Tiffany."

"I know, and though I may not show it, it's one of the things I like about you."

"You mean a great deal to me, Tiffany, so wanting to take care of you comes naturally to me." He touched her cheek. "I know I come across as paranoid sometimes, but the truth is I couldn't bear it if something happened to you. Not when I could've prevented it."

She wrapped her arms around his middle. "Thank you."

His bent down and kissed her. "You're welcome."

Ivan searched her face. "I never want you to feel like I'm smothering you. If I do, just tell me to back off."

"I will," she promised. "I know I've got a few relationship issues that I need to work through."

"Looks like we both have homework in that respect."

"I know I came across as unappreciative, but you make me happy, Ivan, and I love being with you. Never doubt that. "Speaking of covert maneuvers, what other kick-ass stuff can you do?"

Ivan stopped walking and faced her. His fingers slid down the buttons holding her blouse closed as he gazed into her eyes. "I could show you, but we don't have that kind of time."

"I don't know about that. From what I hear there's always time for makeup sex."

Ivan's gaze got heated. "Is that so? Then I guess we'd better get home and find out. If you're wrong, Norma Jean's going to have to settle for a store-bought cake instead."

When they returned to Tiffany's loft, they made it as far as the living room. Grocery bags and clothes were ditched and left wherever they landed as Ivan and Tiffany collapsed onto the couch in a tangle of legs and arms. Their lovemaking was hot and fast. Tiffany held on tight as Ivan drove into her with short, deliberate thrusts. She felt like he was branding her as his, and a primal response bubbled up inside of her. She wanted to feel like she was his in every way.

Seconds later, they both found their release. Spent, they lay there unmoving while their bodies slowly returned to normal.

"Come on, sweetheart," he finally said. "We've got food to fix for Norma Jean's party."

"Do we have to?" Tiffany said. "Can't we just buy her that cake you were talking about earlier and be done with it?"

Ivan stood up and held out his hands to help her up. "I'm not the one going into the line of fire with a store-bought dessert, you are. You know how much Ms. Jeannie loves food from scratch."

"Okay." Tiffany surrendered. "Let's get the eggs and potatoes on first. While they're working up to a boil, we'll take a shower."

"Sounds like a plan, Miss Gentry."

* * *

Tiffany put on a pair of shorts and a halter top. By the time she reentered the kitchen, Ivan was chopping up the potatoes for the potato salad, and the cabbage and carrots were already shredded for the coleslaw.

"You start on the dressing for the slaw, and then we'll get everything put together," he suggested.

While Tiffany put the finishing touches on her dishes, Ivan did some work on his laptop. She was in the bathroom doing her hair when he came up behind her and wrapped his arms around her.

"I have to go," he said, kissing her shoulder. "I'll be back from Vegas late tomorrow evening."

Tiffany stared at their reflection in the mirror. "Okay." She rotated and went into his arms. "Have a safe trip," she murmured. "Call me when you land."

"Roger that." He walked into the living room to retrieve his overnight bag. Tiffany followed behind. They hugged and kissed a final time before Ivan walked out of her door and closed it tightly behind him.

A knot formed in her stomach. How in the world was she going to put on a happy face for tonight's party?

Chapter 15

"And just where have you been?" Norma Jean said without preamble. She took a bag from Tiffany and then stepped aside to let her in.

"I haven't seen you in a month of Sundays," she said.

"You're right. I've been changing out some display cases at the boutique this week to give the place a more summery feel. It's taken up a lot more of my time than I anticipated."

Norma Jean scrutinized her closely. "Really. And what's taking up the rest?"

Tiffany gave it her best performance. It was difficult because she was already missing Ivan like crazy. "Oh, you know, just stuff around the house. Hey, I see Milán and Adrian. I think I'll go say hi." She hugged Norma Jean and made a beeline for her friends.

"House stuff indeed," Norma Jean called after Tiffany. Her husband came up behind her. "What are you up to?"

Norma Jean jumped. "Didn't your mother ever tell you not to sneak up on people?"

He took the tote from his wife. "Jeannie?"

"Honestly, Cliff. Why do you think I'm always up to something?"

Heathcliffe crossed his arms. "You've got to be joking."

"You are a tiresome old man," she complained.

He leaned in and kissed her soundly. "That's not what you said last night."

A gasp escaped her lips. She immediately glanced around to see if they were alone. "Don't go starting stuff you can't finish," she said saucily.

"Take your own advice. Now what were you up to with Tiffany?"

"Nothing. She and I were just visiting. I haven't seen her in a while, you know. Apparently, she's been tied up."

"Good for her." He winked before heading to the kitchen.

"Good indeed," she said, and then broke out into one of her favorite tunes.

Out back, Tiffany found a seat next to Milán and Adrian. They were catching up when Norma Jean came up to their table.

"I was going to have great news, but now my surprise is ruined," she complained.

"What surprise?" Adrian asked.

"I was going to introduce Tiffany to Fernando. He's the nephew of one of my church members."

"She's got an endless supply of those, doesn't she?" Adrian whispered.

His wife nudged him in the ribs.

"Miss Jeannie, I'm not—"

Suddenly everyone was looking at her with interest.

"—sure if I've ever met anyone named Fernando before," she finished, then stood up. "I think I'll get some dessert."

"I'll go with you," Milán said quickly.

"Well, if you're trying to make it look like you're not gaga over Ivan, you're doing a pretty bad job."

She sighed. "Fernando? Really?"

"Tiff, why are you surprised?"

They made their way to the table to fix themselves a plate. Shortly afterward, Adrian joined them.

"So where's Ivan?" he inquired.

Tiffany looked up. "Oh, I heard he's out of town. Your mom said he called to say he wouldn't be able to make it."

Adrian took a bite of his food and then said, "Uh-huh. How are things with you two?"

"You aren't supposed to be eavesdropping on my conversations," Milán admonished.

He looked offended. "Have I ever needed to eavesdrop? Need I remind you that you speak as loud in English as you do in Spanish?"

With her hands on her hips, Milán broke out into a rapid succession of the latter.

"No *comprendo*," he retorted with a boyish grin.

His wife's eyes narrowed. "Oh, you *comprendo* all right."

The two began a conversation that Tiffany wasn't even trying to follow. She caught a word here and there, but was otherwise clueless as to what they were saying.

"Hey," she finally interrupted. "Can we get back to more important stuff…like does your mother know?"

"Why would she?" Adrian turned to his wife. "Unlike women, men don't gossip."

"Since when?" both women said simultaneously.

An hour later, Tiffany told them that she had to run and gave them both a kiss, then went to say goodbye to Norma Jean and Cliff.

"I can't believe you're leaving so soon," Adrian's mother complained. "Things were just getting lively."

"I know, but I'm expecting a call shortly that I have to take…work and all."

"I understand, honey. Too bad you didn't get a chance to meet Fernando. He's such a nice young man."

"I'm sure."

"Summer's the time for romance, which you'd know if you got out of that store every once in a while."

Tiffany hugged her. "I promise I'll get out there soon."

"Mmm-hmm. I'm gonna stop preaching now, but you make sure you take some food home. Men don't like women who are all skin and bones, you know."

"Ms. Jeannie, I'm hardly a twig." Tiffany laughed. "I've got plenty of curves."

Norma Jean kissed her on the cheek. "And you keep them, too. There's nothing wrong with a little bump in the trunk." She laughed.

Tiffany scrunched up her face. "I think it's junk in the trunk, but either way…TMI, Ms. Jeannie."

"Well, whichever one it is, you get my point. It gives them something to hold on to, honey."

"I'm leaving now," Tiffany replied, practically bolting from Norma Jean's side.

Norma Jean's words were still ringing in her ears by the time she got home. Never once did Adrian's mother fail to make her smile. She hoped when she got older that she was as full of love and warmth as Norma Jean.

Ivan hadn't called yet, so she took a quick shower and put on his army shirt. She didn't tie it up this time, so it hung almost to her knees. She climbed into bed and opened up her laptop. She may as well get some work done while she waited.

An hour later, Tiffany had drifted to sleep. The ring of her cell phone startled her. She picked up.

"Hey," she said sleepily.

"Hey, sweetheart."

"How are you?"

"Good. I arrived safely and just got into my room at the hotel."

"I miss you."

"I miss you, too," he replied. "So how was the party?"

Tiffany filled him in on her evening, even about Norma Jean pushing Fernando.

"Another satisfied customer," he joked. "Sounds like a great party. I'm sorry I missed it."

She snorted. "You're sorry."

He chuckled. "I guess I'd better go. We've got an early morning, and from the sounds of it, you need to go to bed."

As if on cue, Tiffany yawned. "Okay."

"Good night, Tiff."

"Good night, Ivan."

"Hey," he said, before she hung up. "What are you wearing?"

"Your army shirt."

"I envy that damned shirt. I bet you look gorgeous."

She smiled at the compliment. "You want me to take a picture and send it to you?"

"Now, that would be nice. That'll give me something to—"

"Ivan," she stopped him. "Were you going to say what I think you were?"

"That depends." His voice deepened. "What were *you* thinking?"

"What I was thinking would start a whole 'nother conversation, so I'm not going to say. You need to go."

"Chicken."

When they hung up, Tiffany took a picture of herself

and sent it. Ivan replied right back that he had it, and that it was going to be a good night for him.

Tiffany laughed aloud, then turned her phone on vibrate before placing it on her nightstand. She was glad that he had called her. She felt much better knowing that he had made it safely. No matter where he was, Tiffany knew she would worry about him. He may have a top-notch, kick-ass team, as he put it, but there was one Ivan Mangum, and he was all hers.

With a satisfied smile, she drifted off to sleep.

Minutes later, the darkness was breached by the bright light from her cell phone. "Blocked" popped up on her screen, and after a few rings it faded away to reveal the wallpaper image of her and Ivan.

Tiffany was in her store the next afternoon when she received a call from Ivan. She let Celeste handle their customer and went to the back room.

"Hi," she said breathlessly. "How are things going?"

"Just fine," he replied. "About to head out to lunch."

"Oh. Well, I'm glad you called me. What time are you coming in this evening?"

"I'm not sure. Can I let you know later?"

"Of course."

A knock sounded at the door. Tiffany sighed. "I'm sorry, but I've got to go. It looks like they need me in the front."

"Sure," he replied in a disappointed voice. "You go back to work. I'll talk to you later."

This time the knock was more insistent.

"Oh, for the love of Pete," she said tersely. "No, wait. Just hold on for a second."

Tiffany stomped across the room and wrenched the door open. She gasped when she saw Ivan on the other side.

"Hey, beautiful."

She was so shocked, she dropped her phone. He reached down and caught it before it hit the floor.

"Ivan," she breathed. She flung herself into his arms. "What… I don't understand. What are you doing here?"

"I was able to wrap things up earlier than expected," he said, hugging her.

"I'm glad you did," she breathed. "I can't believe you're here."

"So." He grinned. "Are you free for lunch?"

Tiffany hugged him tightly. "Of course I'm free."

"Great. Let's go, lady. Daylight's burning."

Ivan took Tiffany to Grant Park. When he parked, Ivan opened the door for Tiffany and then walked around to the trunk of his Range Rover.

"I thought we were going to lunch?"

"We are," he replied, opening the door and taking out a picnic basket.

She laughed. "A picnic? You're taking me on a picnic?"

"Yes." He chuckled. "You don't think I can be romantic when I need to be?"

"On the contrary," she said as they walked. "I'm sure there are many interesting things about you that I don't even know yet."

"Exactly, so come on, woman, and prepare to be impressed."

They found a quiet area in the south rose garden to sit down. Ivan opened the basket and pulled out a plaid blanket. He spread it on the grass while Tiffany set the rest of the things out.

"Wow, you've been shopping," she said, taking out four gourmet sandwiches, several desserts, pasta salad, wine and glasses. "Ivan, there's way too much food in here."

"I like having choices, and since I wasn't sure what you'd like, I wanted to cover all the bases."

She couldn't argue with that. Tiffany chose a Mediterranean sandwich of roasted lamb, lettuce, tomato, feta cheese and an olive tapenade. Ivan picked roast beef and cheese.

"Name one thing about this city that you love the most," he asked a few minutes later.

She thought about it for a moment. "I'd say how well the myriad of cultures, traditions and history blend together. There's literally something for everyone here in the food, the architecture and the people. It's a wonderful place to live, and there's always something new to discover."

"True."

"Where's one place you haven't been that you'd love to go?"

"There are hundreds, believe me, but I'd pick Fiji as being one of the top ten."

"It looks beautiful there," she agreed. "There are so many awe-inspiring places to go in the world that it's hard to pick just a few."

They discussed a few more destinations before Ivan said, "Your birthday is coming up. Any ideas what you'd like to do?"

"Not really. I have this same problem each year. You'd think I'd take the other three hundred and sixty-four to figure it," she joked.

"Would you mind if I picked something for us to do?"

"Of course not. Why would I?"

"I wouldn't want you to think I was being overbearing or anything," he teased.

She tried to swat him, but he moved backward. Not to be outdone, Tiffany lunged for him. He grabbed her around the waist and took her with him. They collapsed back on the blanket, and tussled playfully. Ivan tickled her until she started hiccuping.

"Do you give up?"

"Yes, yes." She laughed. "Scout's honor."

He released her. She sat up, smoothed her clothes down

and then got up. Before Ivan knew what she was up to, Tiffany belted him with a plum and took off running.

He let her get a good distance away before he sprinted after her. Tiffany saw him advancing. She was unable to outrun him, but there was no way she was going to make it easy for him. She darted around bushes, benches, trees, whatever she could find to slow him down, but to no avail. Ivan scooped her up in his arms.

"Scout's honor, huh?"

Tiffany panted from the exertion. "I guess I forgot to mention that I was never a Girl Scout."

Chapter 16

"Mom, you do know that some places actually have carryout? Which means a lot less cleanup later?"

Norma Jean turned to see her son standing at the kitchen entryway. "Boy, when have I ever had carryout for a Sunday dinner?"

Milán, Tiffany and Ivan filed in behind Adrian. After greetings were exchanged, Norma Jean handed each person a dish to take into the dining room.

As usual, Heathcliffe blessed the food. Norma Jean said her usual thanks to the crowd for coming to dinner, and for making her home lively with laughter and love.

"I want you kids to know how much it means to Cliff and me that you all can still take time out of your busy schedules to share an evening with us. It truly means a lot to me." She sniffed. "Especially since I'm not getting any younger."

"Mom," Adrian said, looking over at her with concern. "Why so serious? Is everything okay?"

"Yes, sweetheart. I'm just…overcome with joy tonight. Just seeing you so happy and content—it's all I've ever wanted."

They all sighed with relief.

"Of course, some grandbabies running around would be nice," she added.

"Do we really need to start that again?" Adrian said, on cue.

Since Wednesday was her birthday, Tiffany decided to work Monday and Tuesday and then take the rest of the week off so that she could spend time with Ivan before he left for Venice.

Tuesday afternoon, Ivan told her that he had a surprise for her big day.

"What?"

"Uh-uh. You'll have to wait and see, but we'll need to pack up some things because we'll be gone the rest of the week."

That really got Tiffany's mind buzzing about where the mystery destination could be, but trying to get anything out of Ivan was about as hard as trying to blow a watermelon with a straw. She gave up after the first twenty times of asking, and just packed the things he suggested.

After they got her bags, they drove to Ivan's house to get his things in order. By the time the truck was loaded up that night, Tiffany was exhausted.

"Ivan, where are we going tomorrow?" she pressed when they were in bed that night.

"I'll tell you in the morning."

She tried tickling it out of him, pleading with him and even trying to seduce him. While her efforts put a wide grin on his face, he didn't give in. Turning her back to him, she gave up and went to sleep. She missed the amused look on Ivan's face before he wrapped his arm around her and pulled her up against him. A short time later, they were both asleep.

"Wake up, birthday girl," Ivan whispered into her ear the next morning.

Slowly, Tiffany opened her eyes. She blinked a few times until Ivan came into view.

"Good morning," she said huskily.

"Morning, sweetheart." He kissed her tenderly. "Happy birthday."

"Thank you," she replied, sitting up. "Now where are we going?"

Ivan found her tenacity endearing. He placed a breakfast tray on her lap. He had filled it with her favorites: banana pancakes, turkey sausage and milk. He'd also added fresh flowers from his mother's garden.

He walked over and grabbed his plate that was sitting on the dresser, and then sat on the bed next to her.

"Okay, I'll tell you," he said in between bites of food. "We're going to Lake Geneva. My family has a small cottage there."

"Wisconsin?"

He nodded. "We'll leave as soon as we finish breakfast and get dressed."

"I've never been, but I heard it's great."

"You'll like it," Ivan said confidently.

She leaned over and kissed him. "How can I not? You'll be there with me."

After breakfast, Tiffany went to shower. She was still in there when Ivan returned from taking their breakfast dishes downstairs.

Without warning, he pulled her into his arms and kissed her. It was commanding, firm, all-consuming and intoxicating. He picked her up and carried her back to the bed.

"Ivan, I'm still wet," she exclaimed.

"I don't care." Ivan plunged his tongue into her mouth, and then rained kisses down her face and neck.

Her hands gripped his shoulders, and she gave herself over to his kisses. Minutes later, Ivan was buried to the hilt inside her. He made slow, maddening love to her, and the only thing Tiffany could do was hold on as he painstakingly took them both careening off into a world of mind-blowing orgasms. Tiffany lost count of just how many she had in that short amount of time. Afterward, Tiffany didn't even possess the strength to raise her head off his chest. "This has already been the best birthday I've ever had. How in the world are we going to get up and drive to Lake Geneva?"

"I'm not sure yet," he murmured. "But we've got about twenty minutes to figure it out."

"In that case…can we do that again—all of it?"

A smile of male satisfaction covered his face. "Yes… but not before I've had a chance to recuperate."

But he flipped her over and under him. He kissed her with a newfound strength that left them both breathless.

True to his word, Ivan had them both up, dressed and on the road in twenty minutes. But Tiffany fell back asleep before they had even made it to the interstate.

When she woke up, it was an hour later. She glanced out the window.

The memory of her birthday morning was still fresh in her mind. Sex with Ivan was explosive. Each time left her replete, but wanting more. Just thinking about the last time was enough to stir the embers within her. There was no complicated equation. The more of Ivan she got, the more she wanted. He was addictive. They would be on the road another hour and a half, and yet she was ready to have him take her in the backseat.

Tiffany rotated slightly so that she could observe his

profile. There wasn't one thing about him that she did not find physically desirable. "Ivan," she said slowly.

He glanced over. "Yeah?"

"Can we…stop somewhere?"

"Do you have to use the restroom?"

She reached out and stroked his leg through his jeans. His leg was rock hard. She bit her lower lip. "Not exactly."

"Honey, we'll be there in about ninety minutes."

"I can't wait, Ivan. I was just thinking about earlier this morning and my birthday present and—"

"Ah," he smiled knowingly.

She nodded, moving her hand even lower.

Ivan's jaw clenched. "I do know a place…"

Two hours later, Ivan maneuvered his Range Rover up a winding pebble road. At the top of the hill a log house surrounded on three sides by trees came into view.

"Welcome to Windmere."

Tiffany took in the chestnut-colored A-frame house. She stared at him. "You said it was a *small* cottage."

"It is." He got out and went to retrieve their luggage.

"You know, you and I view the word *small* completely differently." Tiffany got out and went to help with their things. "Call me old-fashioned, but since when does a 'small cottage' describe a six-thousand-square-foot home?"

"It's not that big." He laughed. "Come on."

Following him up the wide steps to the porch, Tiffany noted that it extended around the entire front of the house. Ivan unlocked the front door, and they went in. The lights were already on, and fresh flowers were set in the river-stone fireplace and on the tabletops.

"How did you do this?" she exclaimed.

Ivan motioned for her to follow him. "I had help."

He explained as they walked that the house was built so that the major living areas were at tree level. They walked through the family room to the kitchen. The whole space was engulfed within the trees. She set the bags of groceries onto the dark green-and-black marbled granite counter.

"Looks like the Mangums have commercial-grade kitchens wherever they go."

"What can I say? We love to cook."

They put the groceries away, and then Ivan took her upstairs to his bedroom. Tiffany was in awe. It was like they'd stepped into a tree house. One side of his room had large sliding doors that recessed into the walls so that he had a completely open space that spilled out onto a private balcony. His bed was a massive wooden king-size sleigh bed with dark green bedding. It was a homage to nature, with earth tones and splashes of color as accents. His bathroom was decorated in the same color scheme. There was a round Jacuzzi tub and the same doors that recessed into the wall.

"This is so beautiful, Ivan."

He walked over and wrapped his arms around her. "So are you."

After unpacking, they returned to the kitchen to cook dinner. Tiffany opened a bottle of wine while Ivan prepared steaks to grill. She made a salad, and he took care of baking potatoes. Tiffany found the table linens and set the table, complete with candles and one of the vases of fresh wildflowers. She walked onto the deck and watched him finish up their steaks.

"It must have been wonderful coming up here as a kid."

"Yeah, my parents and grandparents really made sure we had an adventurous childhood. We were always going on fishing trips, campouts and hiking expeditions. We were an outdoorsy group."

"The most outdoorsy thing my family's ever done is the zoo. I think it's great that you have a close-knit family, Ivan."

The longing in her voice was unmistakable. He leaned

over and kissed her. "I can't wait for you to meet them. Of course, my GiGi is going to have my hide for not bringing you to see her sooner."

When dinner was ready, they ate and shared more childhood stories. When they were finished, Ivan cleared their plates. He waved her off when she offered to help.

"You stay there and relax, birthday girl. I'll be right back."

When he returned, he carried a small round cake with candles burning brightly on top. He sang happy birthday, and then Tiffany made a wish and blew out the candles.

"Carrot cake is my favorite. How'd you know?"

"A little birdie told me."

"Does that birdie have a Spanish accent?" She laughed. He smiled. "It's possible."

They moved to the couch. It was a little chilly, so Ivan started a fire. Tiffany sat watching him. When he returned, he carried two wrapped gifts and then sat down beside her. Ivan handed her the boxes.

"Happy birthday, Tiffany."

"Thank you." She unwrapped the first gift and peeked inside the box. She took out a miniature chess set. "Oh, my gosh, Ivan, it's beautiful."

"It's a Thuya wood chess set from Morocco. I thought it would be nice for the Petite Boutique, being that it's the travel-size version." He grinned.

"When did you go to Morocco?"

"I didn't. One of my employees was there on assignment and just got back last week. I asked him to pick it up for me."

"It's perfect," she gushed. "Thank you."

"You're welcome. Here." He handed her the next one.

She pulled the paper off a black box. Tiffany opened it. Her mouth dropped open as she stared at a white-gold and ruby necklace. It was a three-stone setting with each ruby bigger than the last. She touched it lightly with her fingers.

"It's…stunning," she said in a choked voice. "I love it, but it's way too much, Ivan."

He took the necklace out of its case and secured it for her. When it slid down her neck, he settled the rubies into place. "No, it's not. It's your birthday, Tiffany, and I want to spoil you. Do you know how much I'd love to shower you with gifts if you'd let me?"

"Which I won't," she added. "This is too expensive, Ivan."

Ivan dug his heels in. "I'm not taking it back. I should be entitled to splurge on you whenever I want."

Tiffany walked to the hall mirror. He was right; it was perfect. It took considerable effort not to become overwhelmed at the beautiful pendant.

She went back to the couch and sat on his lap. "Thank you for such a special gift, Ivan. It's perfect. My birthday is, too. It's the best one I've had since I don't remember when." Her voice caught in her throat.

He kissed her. "I'm glad, but it's not over yet."

"No? You've already made it a birthday I'll never forget. What else is there?"

"A while ago I was thinking about what I'd like to do for your birthday. Let's just say it involves you and some leftover icing." A wicked gleam entered his eyes. "And it appears we've got plenty of cake to spare."

Tiffany jumped up. "Oh, no, you don't, Ivan Mangum." She screamed when he tried to grab her arm. She yanked it free and took off up the stairs.

"Wait." He laughed. "You haven't seen the best part." He grabbed a spatula and raced after her.

Chapter 17

"I feel bad that we never made it to Lake Geneva," Ivan said when Friday rolled around.

"I'm not." Tiffany smiled, remembering how they'd spent their few days. "I had plenty to keep me occupied." Their getaway in the trees of Wisconsin gave them a true respite from their busy lives. She coveted those few days alone with Ivan. Nothing else mattered. As if the world sensed their need for privacy, not one of them received a phone call, text or even an email while they were at Windmere. They were completely isolated, and content.

The drive to Tiffany's house was solemn. Both were wrapped up in their own thoughts.

In front of her building, they got out of the car and took her things inside. Ivan still needed to go home and get ready for his driver to pick him up later that evening.

Ivan gathered her up in his arms and kissed her soundly. Tiffany threw her arms around his neck and molded herself to him.

When they broke apart, her eyes were wet.

"Hey, I'll be back before you know it."

She could feel his heart beating against her temple. "Trust me. I'll know every second that you're not here."

"I know, sweetheart. I'll miss you like crazy, too. We've got all sorts of stuff to keep us connected— phones, email, video conferencing," he pointed out.

Tiffany tried to put up a happy front, but it was difficult. "None of which will ever replace the real thing."

"Not for me, either, but we'll make the best of it. This time next week I'll be home, and five minutes after that, we'll be in bed making up for lost time."

A genuine smile etched her face. Now that was a picture she could definitely hold on to while he was gone.

"I like the sound of that."

"I thought you might. I've got a surprise for you," he informed her.

"Seriously?"

Ivan sauntered over to one of the bags and retrieved a small, decorative box. He walked back to Tiffany and handed it to her. "Indulge me."

She eyed it excitedly. "Another birthday gift?" This was larger than the last two, and just as nicely decorated.

"You know the present is actually what's inside, and not the box itself," he said with a wry smile.

"Okay, okay." Tiffany untied the ribbon and pulled open the box. Whatever it was was encased in tissue paper. She pulled the paper away, and then held it up.

She glanced up at Ivan with an amused surprise. "It's… a Taser."

"Yeah," he answered, his voice relaying his enthusiasm. "Isn't it cool? It's a C2 model, so it's small and can fit in your purse. I got red. It's stylish and comes with live and practice targets and cartridges, backup battery pack, a holster—"

"It's a Taser," she repeated. "What do you think's going to happen while you're in Venice?"

"I don't know, but whatever it is, you'll be prepared."

Tiffany threw herself into his arms. She hugged him fiercely. "You're a thoughtful and strange man, Ivan Mangum. And if I come up against an unsuspecting bad guy while you're gone, thanks to you, I'll know how to beat him to a pulp, and then fry his ass."

"That's my girl," he said proudly.

They both shared a laugh as Ivan's cell phone rang.

"It's my pilot," he said after he hung up. "We'll be leaving soon. I've got to get going."

Tiffany nodded. They shared another kiss and headed to the door. She followed him to his car.

"Call me and let me know you arrived in Venice safely."

"Roger that." He engulfed her in his arms and gave her one final kiss. "Have fun with the girls."

Tiffany smiled. "You know I'm starting to think you're going to Venice just so you don't have to go on the Love Bird tour."

A shocked expression covered his face. "Would I leave you here to fend for yourself against the Love Broker?"

"Isn't that why you got me the Taser?" she countered.

He laughed heartily at that. She walked him out to the truck. He rolled the window down.

"Have a safe trip," she called out.

He waved. "I will. I'll call you tomorrow when I get in."

"You'd better," she said. Tiffany waved, and remained there until Ivan's Range Rover was out of sight. When it was gone, she turned around and slowly walked back into the house.

It was eight o'clock the next evening when Tiffany got Ivan's call.

"Hey, baby. How are you?"

"Ivan, what are you doing up at this hour? Have you even been to sleep?"

"I slept on the plane. I had to hit the ground running when I got here, so I haven't been to sleep yet. I'm working on the route plan for tomorrow so that I can go over it with my guys in a few hours. There's going to be a lot of traffic due to some huge celebration going on. My client is pretty well-known here, so security is going to be an added challenge."

"Yeah, well, you'd better come back to me in one piece," she warned. "Not even a scratch."

Ivan chuckled. "Yes, ma'am."

She smiled at that.

"What are you up to?"

"Working on sketches for a new line. Ivan, as much as I want to, I'm not keeping you on the phone any longer. You need to get some sleep, especially if it's going to be another long day."

"It is," he agreed.

"I'm glad you called me," she told him. "It's great hearing your voice."

"Yours, too. I'll call you when I can," he promised. "Stay out of trouble."

"Like that's going to be hard to do. You're not here."

They said goodbye and hung up the phone. Tiffany returned to her sketching, but it was difficult. Her mind kept wandering to Ivan. He sounded exhausted, and that worried her.

Ivan threw the papers he was reading across his bed and lay back on his pillows. He'd been in Venice for three days, and it looked as though his week-long assignment was going to turn into two weeks to accommodate a trip to Paris and London. He opened his eyes and glanced at his watch. He had not spoken with Tiffany since the first night he called, but had communicated with her via text messages. His client was a night owl and enjoyed talking business over late dinners or canal rides under the stars with lady friends. There had been at least two other women holding his attention since Ivan's team arrived.

Tonight had no different. His client and his entourage had dined at Naranzaria on the Grand Canal in the heart of the Rialto, followed by music and dancing under the stars and a moonlight stroll. Ivan had followed discreetly behind while other members of his team had been positioned ahead and behind him. His team had had rotations of two twelve-hour shifts. It had made for an extremely long day, but truthfully, Ivan was used to harsher conditions than protecting a wealthy media mogul.

Ivan received an alert in his earpiece about an irate woman approaching. He moved into position in front of his client while another man redirected the other group of partiers. Seconds later she advanced, screaming in Italian and flailing her arms. Ivan spoke to her in Italian to try to defuse the situation. She was having none of it. He tried to calm her down, but it wasn't working. By then the men behind him had escorted their client and his companion into an awaiting limo. The woman tried to sidestep Ivan, but her efforts were futile. He blocked her path until the sedan sped off.

Livid at not achieving her goal, she took her wrath out on Ivan. She screamed obscenities at him for thwarting her ability to give her ex-lover a piece of her mind.

Ivan apologized and released her. She threw up her hand in an unladylike gesture and stomped off.

He kept his line of sight on her until she disappeared, before doubling back to rendezvous with his team. It was then he received word that their client was retiring for the evening. Gratefully, Ivan dismissed all but a select group and called it a night.

A few hours later, Ivan woke up from a troubled sleep. He glanced at the clock on his nightstand. It was four in the morning. He got off the bed and padded into the bathroom to splash cold water on his face. He heard his phone chirping in the other room. He hurried to pick it up. "Mangum."

"Are you busy?"

"Hey, Mike. No more than usual at this hour," he said with humor. "What's up?"

"Sorry for the delay, but I've got that number you were looking for."

"Great. Send it to my phone."

"No need," he replied. "You already know it."

When his buddy told him the name of the caller, Ivan swore under this breath.

"Thanks, Mike. I owe you one."

He set his phone back on the table and then sat heavily on the bed. It would appear that Cole's warning had come back to bite him in the ass, and he wasn't happy about it at all, but he would have to deal with it when he got off assignment.

He placed a call to his assistant. He was not surprised that he picked up on the second ring. When he was in the field, Curtis always answered his phone in case Ivan needed administrative support.

"Hi, Curtis, I need you to call ahead and get Windmere ready for me, and book a flight from there to Madison for next week. No, I'm not staying. Book the return flight for an hour after I get there."

"Of course, sir."

He thanked him and hung up. After that he dialed Tiffany.

"Hey," she said breathlessly. "How are you?"

"I'm well. Sorry I haven't called in a few days."

"It's okay, Ivan. I understand. At least you're able to text."

"I know it hasn't been ideal." He sighed. "And unfortunately, my assignment's been extended another week."

Tiffany's heart constricted at hearing that Ivan's trip was going to be longer than a week. She wasn't thrilled to hear the news that he wouldn't be coming home just yet, but it was his job, his career. She understood.

"You're right, that's not ideal news, but we knew going in that it was a possibility."

He was silent for a moment, and then said, "I…miss you, Tiff. I can't begin to express just how much."

Starlight could not have eclipsed her smile. "I miss you, Ivan. And you're right. Sometimes words aren't good enough."

He had to go so they said goodbye. After Tiffany hung up, she sat there a moment. She meant what she said. She was disappointed, but would support him any way she could. His business was as important to him as the Petite Boutique was to her. Somehow, they would make the distance work when he had to travel for business.

Restless, Tiffany decided to focus her energy on her business. She would remain busy to keep from obsessing over how long Ivan would be gone. A sigh of relief escaped her lips. She had a plan.

A week later, Tiffany's shop was bustling with clientele.

"I guess that new coupon campaign is helping," she told Celeste.

"I'd say your idea paid off big-time," she agreed. "It's a madhouse in here."

When Tiffany got home that night, she texted Ivan. She waited for a while, but when he didn't respond, she figured he was busy. *Good night, Ivan.* With a sigh, Tiffany began working on her website. When her doorbell rang, she set her laptop on the couch and padded to the door. When she looked through the peephole, Tiffany let out a scream. She yanked the door open and jumped into Ivan's arms, hugging him fiercely.

"What are you doing here?" she shrieked. She kissed him repeatedly.

"Hey, sweetheart."

"Oh, my God, I'm so happy to see you," she cried. "I didn't expect you to come here straight from the airport."

"Why wouldn't I? Damn," he said lowering her to the floor.

"What's wrong?"

"I forgot something," he replied, and then kissed her a final time. "I'll be right back."

"Wait. Here." She handed over her house keys. Before Tiffany could say another word, he'd left. Confused, she shut the door.

Tiffany fell asleep waiting for Ivan to return. She was woken up by a soft pressure on her cheek. She opened her eyes to find Ivan tracing a thumb down her cheek.

"Ivan Mangum, where in the world did you go?"

He held up a bag from Oberweiss Dairy. "I got your favorite, Turtle Candy sundae."

"That's what you forgot?" she said. "You're insane. There was no way ice cream was more important than seeing you."

"Does that mean you don't want it?" He moved the bag away.

"Don't be silly." Tiffany sat up and leaned against the headboard. She held her hand out for the bag.

Ivan took off his shoes and got into bed beside her. She dived into her treat while he sipped his chocolate malt.

"This was a wonderful surprise."

She laughed, but then turned serious. "Do you know how much I missed you?"

He sat his malt down on her nightstand and faced her.

He searched her face for a few moments. "Are you sure that's not the sundae talking?"

"You're impossible." She hugged him, and then sat her ice cream on the other nightstand. "You're a fool if you think that I'd prefer any ice cream over you."

"Is that so?"

"Yes, I care about you," she said seriously.

"That's good to know, because I care about you, too. Now, there's just one more thing."

Her smile faltered. "Is it good news?"

"Besides my wanting to tear your clothes off? Yes. I'm off for a while. You've got me all to yourself. No distractions."

She relaxed. "I can handle that. Now, about that tearing my clothes off thing…when do you start?"

He kissed her. "Well, earlier I told you I'd be buried inside you five minutes after I got home."

"Yeah, you bungled that with the Oberweiss run," she said.

He moved forward until she was lying down on the bed, and he was hovering over her. "I guess now I'm going to have to make up for lost time."

"Yeah," she said enticingly. "I guess you will."

Chapter 18

"Tiff, I have to tell you something—and you aren't going to like it."

Ivan and Tiffany were lying on the couch a few days later, watching the fire blaze in the hearth.

"Okay." She sat up, instantly alert. "What is it?"

"I found out who the blocked calls were coming from."

Tiffany pushed up from his chest and sat back. "Who?"

Ivan paused. "Debra."

She stared at him. "Excuse me? Why in the world would she call me and keep hanging up?"

"The only thing I can come up with now is that she was trying to run you off."

"From what?"

Ivan braced himself. "Me."

"Wait a minute, you told me that you two were over years ago."

"That's true," he replied.

"Well, apparently not, Ivan, if she's trying to harass me via cell phone."

"As far as I'm concerned, the only connection between us is her dead husband and the promise I made to help while she got on her feet."

"Well, obviously she isn't just interested in your support."

"It's irrelevant what she's interested in. That's all I've given her, and will ever give her. That, and I recommended that she speak with a therapist to work through some of her issues."

Tiffany's eyes widened. "Oh, this just gets better and better. This is what Cole meant, wasn't it? Debra wants you, and has no qualms about doing whatever she can to keep you near."

"You're right," he finally said. He shook his head. "I didn't see it at first, but I did eventually. In fact, I told her that I was stopping my support in one month. My company has done some business with a client near her. I put in a good word, and she has an interview. That's it for my help. Whatever happens now, she's on her own."

"When did you tell her all this?"

"A while ago."

Tiffany looked surprised. "Really? You told her before you found out she was the one calling me?"

"Yes."

The anger left her instantly. Tiffany linked her hands in his. "Thank you."

He touched her cheek. "You're welcome."

"Ivan, listen to me. You've been kind, beyond generous and a true friend to her late husband. Especially considering the circumstances of his marriage to Debra, but now she's using your compassion against you. I can deal with the fact that she blew up my phone trying to run me off, but that's not going to happen. I'm here to stay, and the emotional blackmail that she's been putting you through has to stop."

"I don't care about me, Tiffany. I can handle it, but her harassing you is unacceptable. You and your safety are my main priority."

"I understand her motivation, but I'm not about to share you with any woman."

He stepped closer. "Say that again."

Tiffany poked him in the chest. "I won't share you. Okay, maybe with your mom and grandmother, but that's it—only women who are related to you, and then only conditionally."

He hugged her tightly. "I'm not going to share you, either," he informed her. "When my buddy told me who'd been calling you, I booked a flight to Madison. I'm going up there to settle this thing once and for all."

"Correction. *We* are going. We're going to sit down and discuss this like three rational adults."

"And if that doesn't work?" he inquired.

"Then I'm whipping out the Cane-Fu."

They both started laughing at Tiffany's declaration. Ivan gazed into her eyes.

"Are we good?"

"You mean, am I mad at you for your stalker ex-girlfriend prank-calling me?"

"Uh, yes."

"No, I'm not. I'm not threatened or jealous with regards to Debra. She will never come between us," Tiffany said confidently. "We'll handle the situation—together."

"That seems to be how we function best, isn't it?"

"You got it, Mangum."

He picked her up and headed for the stairs.

"Where are you taking me?" she demanded.

"To my bedroom. We have some makeup sex to get to."

"But Ivan, I already said I'm not mad at you."

His gaze could have singed her hair. "Well, I suggest you pretend."

When they pulled up to Debra's house, she came running out.

"Ivan, what a nice surprise," she gushed. "Why didn't you tell me you were coming?"

Tiffany walked up behind Ivan. She stopped next to him.

All pretense of calm left Debra's face. "What is she doing here?"

"Debra, I'd like you to meet Tiffany—my girlfriend."

She eyed Tiffany. "I know who she is. I saw her on your social-media sites—" She stopped short.

Ivan frowned.

"Hello, Debra," Tiffany said.

Debra ignored her. Instead, she turned to Ivan. "I'd ask you to come in, but the house is a mess."

"We're not staying," he replied. "We need to talk. Would you mind if we sat on the porch?"

"No, of course not." She turned around and headed back to the house. Ivan and Tiffany followed.

Debra sat down. She regarded Tiffany. "So, why are *you* here?"

"I came with Ivan, of course."

"Yes, but why? I'm sure what Ivan and I have to discuss can't be your business."

"*He* is my business." Tiffany replied.

"For the moment, it seems."

"Enough," Ivan snapped. "This isn't a social call. You've been calling Tiffany's cell phone, and it's going to stop. She's done nothing to you, and I won't have her harassed like that."

Debra shrugged. "I don't know what you're talking about."

Ivan pulled out his cell phone and hit a button. Debra's house phone started ringing.

Ivan's expression turned glacial. "You want to try that again?"

"Fine. I did call her. Can you imagine how I felt seeing her all over your social-media pages? I admit it was wrong, but I wanted to make sure she was aware of the... understanding between us."

"There is no understanding between us, Debra. That ended the moment you threw me over for Brian."

"You're right. It was wrong of me, and I'm sorry I hurt you. I loved my husband, Ivan, but he's gone. You're the only connection to him that I have left. He spoke about you so much, and he loved you like a brother," she cried. "It was only natural that I'd turn to you during my time of grief."

"Does manipulating someone qualify as grief?" Tiffany inquired.

Debra turned on her. "What do you know about it? How dare you come in here and judge me."

"I know that you used Ivan for financial support, while purposely distorting his kind heart and sense of obligation as some rekindled love for you. Go ahead," Tiffany demanded. "Tell me I'm wrong."

Debra's face turned a mottled red. She lunged for Tiffany, but Ivan was faster. He jumped up and blocked her path.

"I want you off my property," Debra said to Tiffany, "or so help me, I'll have you arrested for trespassing."

"*We* are leaving," Ivan said. "I'm done, Debra. Our financial arrangement has concluded. Don't contact me or Tiffany ever again. Do you understand?"

"You promised," she cried. "You promised that you'd

take care of me, you promised that you'd be there for me, and this is how you repay me? How you repay *him?*"

Ivan was barely able to contain his anger. "Tiffany," he said calmly. "Can you give us a minute?"

"Sure."

After Tiffany headed back to the car, Ivan turned back to Debra, and any semblance of civility was gone. His eyes were bright with barely restrained hostility. Debra wrenched herself out of his grasp and backed up a few paces, actually looking frightened.

"We've settled all our debts to each other, Debra. I meant what I said about not contacting me or Tiffany ever again. If there's so much as one hair that gets mussed on her head, I will know it was you, or that you had a hand in it. And if that day comes—"

"You'll what?" she taunted. "Call the police on me for harassing your girlfriend? I'll deny it."

"I don't need police," he said coldly. "There is nowhere on this planet you can hide that I won't find you, Debra. And I hope for your sake you're smart enough not to ever want that day to arrive."

Debra stood rooted to the spot. Her eyes bugged out in fear.

He leaned closer. "Do you understand me?"

She could only nod.

Without another word, Ivan strode back to the car. He got in and kissed Tiffany.

"Let's go home," was all he said before he put the car in gear and drove off.

The next night, Tiffany and Ivan were at his house watching a movie when his cell phone rang.

Tiffany glanced over. "Work?"

"Yep, I promise it won't be long." He stepped away to take the call.

Fifteen minutes passed, and Ivan still had not returned. Tiffany got up and went looking for him. She found him outside on the patio standing in the darkness.

"Hey, what are you doing out here?"

He didn't turn around. "Thinking."

Tiffany walked over. "Ivan, what's wrong?"

He took her hand in his. "I just got offered the chance to take on a client who'll be working out of the country for several months in Dubai. He asked for me specifically. Apparently, I came highly recommended. He said he heard I was the best, and he only wants the best. You know what the irony is? I once thought something like this was a dream job for me."

"Why?"

"Because the money I'd make on this one client would allow me to expand my business interests internationally, which could mean a lot of follow-up work, if all went well."

Tiffany's heart dropped to her stomach. She stood there for a minute before she spoke.

"Are you going to take the job?"

"Before, I would've accepted on the spot, but things have changed, Tiff."

He turned to face her. Though it was dark, his hand went right to her face. He grazed her cheek with his fingers. "You're in my life now. What we have is important to me, Tiffany. Whatever decision I make affects you now, too."

His words sent her heart soaring. "Is this job going to be dangerous?"

He grasped her hand, and she followed him back inside. Ivan turned off the television, and they went upstairs to his room. They sat on the bed facing each other.

"Sweetheart, there's an element of danger in the majority of the jobs I do. It only takes a split second for something to go wrong. I won't lie and say that this assignment won't have a heightened level of security."

She nodded. "When do you have to let him know?"

"I have forty-eight hours to get back to him."

Tiffany's expression fell. "Ivan, that doesn't give you much time."

"I agree, but what I really need to know is what you think about the offer. Where are you on this?"

Tiffany was thoughtful for a moment. "Honestly, I think it sounds like an incredible opportunity for you and your company, Ivan. I think you should seriously consider it."

He placed a hand under her chin and tilted her face to meet his. "Even if it would mean leaving you?"

She nodded. "I don't like the idea of you leaving, whether it's a short or long-term assignment, or the possibility that you're in mortal danger," she admitted. "But I will support whatever decision you make. I told you before, we're in this together, Ivan. No matter what you choose."

Somber, they both agreed to set it aside for the night.

Troubled, Tiffany called Milán the next day and told her about Ivan's job offer. She immediately instructed her to come over.

When she arrived, her friend hugged her. "I'm glad you're here. Jeannie is here, too," she whispered. "Don't worry, I've made a pitcher of margaritas, and Adrian's at Justin's watching a basketball game."

"Hi, lovebug," Norma Jean said when Tiffany came out onto the patio. She pulled Tiffany into her arms. "Milán told me what's going on."

"I figured you didn't want to repeat it again," her friend said, by way of an apology.

"It's fine," Tiffany told her.

They had already told Norma Jean that they were dating. She had taken it well, even the part about being kept in the dark for a while.

The group stretched out on lounge chairs while they sipped their drinks.

"The biggest question is whether you can be without him for several months. It may start out as two to three, but what if it goes longer? Would you be okay with that?" Milán asked.

"I agree that it would seem like forever, but in reality, his being away wouldn't be any different than if he were still on active duty in the army. Both would mean a long separation, and Ivan being in harm's way."

Norma Jean observed her for a minute. "You really do care for him, don't you?"

Tiffany replied instantly. "Yes. Ivan means the world to me, Jeannie. I can't imagine my life without him."

"Then don't despair, honey. It will work out. Remember, the heart wants what the heart wants. You should always listen to what it's telling you. Most people run into trouble when they don't follow that simple tenet. You've got a great man, Tiffany, and he would do anything for you. That isn't something people find every day. You've got to hold on to it—and cherish it."

Tiffany wiped the tears from her eyes. "I know." She got up. "Thank you both for being here and listening to me. I'm sorry, but I have to go. I've got something I need to do."

"We're here anytime you need us, *chica. Te amo.*"

"I love you, too, Lani. You, too, Jeannie."

In the car, Tiffany called Ivan and asked him to meet her at Buckingham Fountain in an hour.

Arriving early, Tiffany had a chance to watch the water show that occurred every twenty minutes. She tilted her head back to see the center jet shoot water in a one-hundred-and-fifty-foot vertical line.

She sensed Ivan before she saw him. "Beautiful, isn't it?"

"Yes, it's one of the things I love most about the city." He observed her profile. "How's your day been?"

"About as good as yours, I suppose," she replied.

Taking her hand in his, Ivan began walking. "So what's on your mind?"

She got straight to the point. "Ivan, I think you should take the job."

He stopped and faced her. "Tiffany…are you sure?"

"Yes, I'm sure. Ivan, we're a team. I support what's important to you. If our roles were reversed, and I was the one having to go away for my job, I know you'd be in my corner one hundred percent. I want to do the same for you. I'll be here waiting for your safe return—no matter what."

Ivan searched her face. "Sweetheart, as long as I have your support, that's all I need." He kissed her solemnly. "I'll get time off, so I'll be back as soon as I can manage it."

"You'd better," she said tearfully.

They resumed walking.

"When will you let your client know?"

"I'll call him tomorrow morning. I don't want anything taking away from our night together."

"How long do we have?"

"Probably just a few days."

She nodded. "I guess we'd better make the most of them."

"We'll do whatever you want to do," he promised her. "Name it."

"I'd like to go back to Navy Pier."

He grinned. "The Ferris wheel?"

"The Ferris wheel."

They took a trolley ride to the pier. Tiffany felt like a kid again when Ivan escorted her into their compartment on the ride. She held on tightly to his arm as the ride lurched forward, and they were airborne. When they got off, Ivan took her to the carousel and set her atop an inanimate horse. With each revolution of the ride, Tiffany giggled like a schoolgirl.

When it was time to go home, Ivan walked her back to her car.

"Thanks for a lovely evening." She leaned up to kiss him. "I had fun."

"Me, too."

She started her car. "Are you coming back to my house?"

He leaned down so that they were at eye level. "Do you want me to?"

Tiffany cocked her head to the side. "Of course. When don't I want to sleep with you?"

That made him grin. "I'm not in the habit of not giving my lady what she wants."

"Good to know. Your lady will be in the bed wearing nothing but a smile. Don't keep her waiting."

With that, Tiffany sped away from the curb and down the street.

Chapter 19

"You look amazing," Ivan assured Tiffany from the doorway, where she was getting ready.

"I'm meeting your grandmother, Ivan. I'm too nervous to look amazing." On their last night together, Tiffany decided to invite a few guests over to her house for a bon voyage party.

He sauntered into the bedroom. "My grandmother won't bite. You'll be fine."

"I'll try, but your grandmother blesses you and Cole out at the drop of a dime. What will she do to me?"

"That's different. Cole and I are her grandsons."

"Exactly. You two are family. What's she going to do to a person who isn't related to her by blood?"

"She will be on her good behavior. Now stop worrying or I'll have to…relax you."

"Oh, no, you don't." She sidestepped him. "We're not going to be late for your going-away party. Not gonna happen, Romeo."

He stalked her with slow, predatory steps. His eyes were alight with mischief. Tiffany started to giggle and backed up.

"Stop it. I mean it, Ivan. I've got to go check on dinner."

She took off running out the bedroom before he could stop her.

When Ivan reached the kitchen, Tiffany was checking on her roasted lamb.

"I don't know why you didn't let me hire waitstaff to help you."

"Because this is my first dinner party in who knows how long. I wanted to do it all myself," she explained. "It's important to me."

"Okay," he replied. "But you'd better not be too tired to wish me a bon voyage later. As a matter of fact, we've got time now to—"

Tiffany glared at him. "No, we don't."

Luckily for her, the doorbell rang. They opened the door together to greet their first guest. Cole entered and escorted their grandmother inside.

Ivan hugged her and took her shawl. He wrapped his free arm around Tiffany.

"GiGi, this is Tiffany Gentry. Tiffany, this is my grandmother, Cecile Mangum."

Tiffany reached out to shake her hand. "I'm delighted to meet you, Mrs. Mangum."

"It's wonderful to meet you, too, Tiffany—finally." She directed the last word at Ivan. "I've heard so much about you, and I can see now that Ivan and Cole didn't exaggerate. You are lovely."

Tiffany blushed. "Thank you." She showed Ivan's grandmother to the couch while Ivan went to hang up her shawl.

Norma Jean and Heathcliffe came in next, and then Milán and Adrian. Ivan introduced the group to his grandmother.

"It's wonderful to finally meet another member of Ivan's family," Norma Jean said, sitting next to Cecile. "You have wonderful grandsons, Ms. Cecile."

"I agree, dear, but they're a handful." She chuckled. "Just like their father."

Milán found Tiffany in the kitchen as she was taking some appetizers out of the refrigerator.

"I've got that," she said, scooting Tiffany out of the way. "You go help entertain your guests."

"Are you sure?" Tiffany said uncertainly.

"Of course. Now get going."

Tiffany hugged her friend and returned to the living room. She sat on the arm of Ivan's chair. He placed an arm loosely around her.

"Tiff, Ms. Cecile was just telling us a lively story about the first time Ivan tried to cut his own hair." Norma Jean laughed.

"Honey, it looked like he had two Mohawks on the top of his head," his grandmother said.

"Mom was furious," Cole added. "We were scheduled to get family portraits taken the next afternoon."

"Oh, no," Tiffany said. "What happened?"

"My mother had me wait for my father in the foyer to make sure he saw me. When he got home—"

"The look on his face was priceless," Cole said. "First he grounded Ivan for messing with his hair clippers, and then he had to sit there while Dad gave him a buzz cut. It was hilarious."

"Not to Mom," Ivan said drily. "Just seeing those pictures makes her mad all over again."

Milán entered with a platter of assorted appetizers. Everyone dug into the pinwheels and puffed pastries with gusto.

"Would anyone like a drink?"

Ivan took drink orders, and Adrian got up to help him.

When the kitchen timer went off, Tiffany excused herself to go check on the meal.

"Need some help?" Norma Jean said from the doorway.

"Yes, thank you. Everything is ready. I'll let the lamb sit for a few minutes while we put everything on the table."

In addition to roast lamb, which was Ivan's favorite, she had also made garlic mashed potatoes, roasted whole green beans with pine nuts and homemade garlic parmesan knots. All eight of them sat down at the dining table. Heathcliffe said a special grace to bless the food and Ivan's journey. Everyone said, "Amen," and began passing dishes around.

As was the norm at Norma Jean's house, the dinner conversation was lively. Cecile was fascinated by the tale of the Love Broker, and how successful Norma Jean had been at making love matches for Adrian and his friends.

"Have you breathed a sigh of relief yet?" Ivan whispered in Tiffany's ear.

"Sort of," she admitted. "I just wanted tonight to be superspecial for you."

He leaned in for her ears only. "Sweetheart, this dinner is absolutely perfect. Having our friends and family here is awesome, and I'm truly appreciative of your hard work in making this happen, but the superspecial part of this night is being able to share it with you."

That declaration was enough to make Tiffany lose her composure. She politely excused herself and walked into her room and shut the door.

Ivan would leave tomorrow, and it had suddenly become real that he was leaving and would be gone for months. She didn't know when he'd get a chance to come home to visit. Ivan was the most important thing in her life, and all bravado aside, her heart was breaking at the loss.

She was still trying to get it together when Ivan tapped on the door a few minutes later. He opened it and poked his head in.

When he saw her crying, he was at her side in an instant. He knelt down beside her.

"Tiff, what's wrong? Are you okay?" he said with concern. He placed a hand on both her knees. "Talk to me, are you ill? Was it something you ate?"

"That's the most beautiful thing anyone has ever said to me," she said.

Ivan stared at her in confusion. "What?"

"You said that all you needed to make your night special was me. Nobody has ever said anything like that to me before."

He relaxed. "Tiffany, look at me."

She raised bloodshot eyes to meet his.

"Baby, just because I'll be on the other side of the world doesn't mean I won't be able to tell you how I feel about you, and how important you are to me."

"I know, but…it won't be the same. You won't be here *with* me." She sniffed and blew her nose.

"True, but the sentiments won't change, sweetheart. I care about you—two inches away, or two million."

A light rap sounded at the door. "Tiffany?" Milán said hesitantly. "Are you okay? I don't mean to interrupt, but Ivan's grandmother is asking about dessert. She wants to know if you have stuff to make a chocolate sundae."

Tiffany burst out laughing. "Come in, Lani," she called out.

Milán opened the door an inch at a time.

Ivan helped Tiffany to her feet, and then faced Milán. "Would you mind helping Tiffany? I'm going to go fix the Grand Dame a sundae. She's stuck on them right now, and nothing else will do."

"Sure," she said, going to her friend. "We'll be out shortly."

Ivan cast a glance at Tiffany a final time before he left.

Milán hugged her friend. "It'll be okay," she soothed. "You'll see."

Tiffany blew her nose again, and dabbed at her eyes. "Is it bad?"

Her friend looked her over. "Yes. You do look like a train wreck, but we can fix it," she said confidently.

By the time the two friends returned, everyone was back in the living room holding dessert plates. Everyone except Ivan's grandmother. She had a dessert dish filled to the hilt with ice cream slathered in chocolate, with a cherry on top. She was blissfully happy.

Ivan got up and walked over to Tiffany. "How are you feeling?" he said with concern.

"I'm fine," she replied. "How do I look?"

"As beautiful as you did a few minutes ago."

"Ha." She snorted. "My nose was running, my eyes were the color of lobster and my cheeks were puffy."

He leaned in closer. "True," he said, for her ears only, "but I still wanted to lean you over and—"

"Ivan," she gasped, blushing.

He kissed her rosy nose. "What? I think you're sexy no matter how you look."

Milán and Norma Jean exited the kitchen with two trays of champagne flutes. They handed each person a glass as Tiffany stepped in front of the crowd.

"First, I'd like to say thank you all for coming tonight to support Ivan as he embarks on a new and exciting project. I know it means a great deal to him, as it does me, to have you all here to bid him farewell, good fortune and a safe journey on his trip to Dubai. I hope this trip brings Ivan and Mangum and Associates much success now and in the future. So raise your glasses with me and wish Ivan well."

Everyone clinked their glasses. Next Cole came up and gave a toast.

"Ivan, I know I joke around a lot, but you're much more than just my big brother. You're my best friend. I look up to you, I respect and value your opinion, and I'm very proud of your accomplishments. Besides that, that scowl of yours never fails to send the ladies running my way instead of yours." Seeing the look on Ivan's face, he added, "Except one."

The group laughed.

"Here's to you, Ivan. I love you, I'll miss you, and I wish you the best of luck."

Each person took a turn saying kind words about Ivan and wishing him well. Even Cecile stood up and slowly walked over to stand near Ivan and Tiffany. She tapped her grandson on the shoulder and said, "I like her, honey. You did a good job. She's a little on the small side, but she's got good hips so she should have no problem cranking out the next generation of Mangums."

Tiffany blushed almost as deep as the red dress she was wearing. Quickly, Ivan cleared his throat and thanked everyone for coming to see him off.

Excusing herself, Tiffany headed back to the kitchen to get more champagne. When she got there, she placed her hands up to her heated cheeks.

"Well, at least she likes you," Ivan said from the doorway.

"Thank God I'm built to crank out baby Mangums," she said, blushing all over again. "She may have just knocked Norma Jean off her pedestal for who can say something to shock the most people in a single night."

Ivan strode over and picked her up.

"What are you doing?" she hissed. "Put me down."

"Not till you say, 'Ivan, you were right, your grandmother likes me.'"

"I'm not saying that."

He started to tilt her.

"Okay, okay. Ivan, you were right. Your grandmother likes me."

He lowered her to the ground, but still kept her in his arms. "See, was that so hard? Plus, she's right, you know."

"About what?"

"You do have good bone structure." He moved the palm of his hand over her stomach. "When the time comes, I'm sure you'll have no problem birthing one of my babies."

She shoved him. "You're not funny, Ivan Mangum. I'm going to pay you back for this," she promised him before hurrying back to their guests.

When Ivan came out, he went straight to Tiffany's side and placed a possessive arm around her waist.

"Thanks for being a part of this celebration. Your kind words tonight just reconfirm that we're all connected in some way by love, respect and admiration. I made a promise to Tiffany that I'm coming back to her safe and in one piece, and I meant it."

"You'd better if you know what's good for you," his brother chimed in.

As the party wound down, Tiffany was in the kitchen cleaning up when Norma Jean wandered in and walked over to Cole, who was making a plate to take home.

"Do you need help with anything, Cole?"

"No, thanks, Ms. Jeannie. I'm good."

"This was such a wonderful party. I noticed your girlfriend wasn't here. Did she have to work late?"

Tiffany smiled. She knew where this was going.

"Hardly," Cole said drily. "I don't have one, and that's the way I like it."

"You don't say?"

"Mom," Adrian practically yelled from the doorway. "There you are. I've been looking all over for you."

"I'm hard to miss, honey. I've just been in here talking to Cole."

"Splendid, but it's time to go," he said, before taking her arm and leading her out.

Cole and their grandmother were the last to leave.

"Thanks, little brother. I appreciate everything you've done for me," Ivan said to Cole.

"Hey, that's what I'm here for, right? I've always got your back."

"I'm going to miss you."

"Me, too," Cole replied.

They hugged and clapped each other on the back. "Cole..."

"You don't have to say it, Ivan."

"Yes, I do," he said with emotion. "Look out for her. I...I need to know that she's safe."

"Of course I will, Ivan. As if she were my own sister."

Ivan nodded. Relief suffused his face. "That's good to know, because she will be someday."

The two brothers shared a moment of understanding before Cole moved off to say good-night to Tiffany.

Ivan took the opportunity to say goodbye to his grandmother.

"It's been a hell of a night," she said, when he came to her side.

"That it has."

"She's a great girl, Ivan. I mean that. I can tell she doesn't take any crap from you, either. That makes me like her even more."

He shook his head. "Is that so?"

"You know me—I like women with spunk. She looks like she gives as good as she gets. I meant what I said earlier. I think she'll do nicely—and not just to dip your cone in, either."

"GiGi," Ivan warned.

"Don't GiGi me," she said, raising herself up to her full height. "You'd better not go over to Dubai and get yourself hurt. That would really piss me off."

Ivan gave his grandmother a big hug. He kissed her cheek. "I wouldn't dream of it."

He saw his family to the car. When he came back in, Tiffany wasn't in the living room. He locked the door and turned out the lights.

Ivan reached her bedroom door and stopped short. The entire room was engulfed in candlelight. Tiffany was kneeling in the center of the bed waiting for him, her body shimmering with incandescent light. The cream-colored lace nightie she wore teased him with what was to come. Ivan was struck with the reverence of it all. It felt almost like his wedding night. His gaze traveled over the woman who had come to mean the world to him in such a short amount of time. Nothing could have prepared him for how his five-foot-two-and-a-half-inch beauty could have captured his heart so completely.

He fought to contain the emotion bubbling up inside. He had to be strong...for both of them.

"Words fail me."

Her face lit up at his compliment. "I was thinking the same thing."

Ivan walked to the bed. He sat down at the foot. "I could stare at you all night."

"Not all night," she teased.

"Thank you," he said humbly.

"For what?"

"Where do I start? For your thoughtful words earlier, for throwing me a spectacular party, for...tonight."

"When I first saw you, I remember thinking that you were an Army of One, and it's true. I know you'll protect me and keep me safe from harm—and I want to do the same for you."

"You do, Tiffany. I recall thinking that with you, I could be myself. I can let my guard down because you've got my back. You're the one looking out for me."

"I take my job seriously," she reminded him.

Tiffany reached up and began to unbutton his shirt. When she was finished, she slid it off his shoulders. He tossed it on the floor. She knelt forward and unbuckled his belt and then unzipped his pants. Ivan got up and stepped out of them, and then his boxer briefs. Totally devoid of clothing, he stood there.

Tiffany shook her head in wonder. "You're magnificent."

As if he had all the time in the world, Ivan slid the straps to Tiffany's nightgown down one at a time. The nightgown fell to a pool around her stomach. She was wearing the ruby necklace he'd given her. He reached out and fondled the three gemstones. She was wearing his heart, his mind and his soul, and didn't even know it.

"So are you."

They made love slowly, and with infinite tenderness. Ivan caressed every inch of Tiffany, as if committing her to memory. He coaxed her body to a fever pitch, and when they finally came together, seconds later, Tiffany erupted with pleasure almost instantly.

Ivan felt her squeezing him tight and holding him in a honeyed embrace. He rolled her over and on top of him. From his vantage point, he could have full access to her body, and when he slipped his hand between her legs, his ministrations awarded him the best view of her ecstatic second release. He closed his eyes and savored the feel of her holding him inside of her. Surrounded by warmth. Protected.

This time, when Ivan felt his control ebbing, it was Tiffany who lured him over the edge with her sweet words of affection.

"Let go, Ivan. I've got you."

He reached up and slowed the rhythmic moving of her hips. "You got me, baby?"

Her eyes never left his. "Always," she promised.

Tiffany felt his body clench, and then Ivan tumbled into oblivion. Seconds later, she joined him a third time before collapsing onto his chest. They held each other tightly, reverently, and then slipped away into an exhausted slumber.

The morning came too soon, and with it the painful reminder that they were out of time. Like before, they said their goodbyes, and then Tiffany followed Ivan out to his Range Rover.

He laid his forehead on hers. "I'll call you as soon as I get there," he promised.

"You'd better," she said tearfully. "No matter what time it is."

He picked her up and held her. Both were oblivious to the people staring as they walked by. They kissed a final time before Ivan climbed up into his truck and drove off. She watched until he was gone from sight before walking with heavy steps back into her apartment. She went back to the bed and crawled under the covers. She hugged the bedding tightly, Ivan's scent still fresh.

Somehow Tiffany settled into daily life without Ivan. She learned to cope for the first month with text messages, video chats and telephone calls, but the craving she felt for Ivan was becoming tangible. Her friends tried to get her mind off his absence by inviting her out as often as they could. As he'd promised, Cole kept in constant contact with her. They were having lunch downtown one day when she said, "Have you spoken to Ivan lately?"

"Yep, I spoke with him a week ago."

"How'd he seem to you?"

"Better now," he replied. "I told him if he's going to get his ass kicked every time he goes out of town, he really should think about lowering his health-insurance deductible."

Tiffany's fork clattered onto her plate. "What?"

Cole's gaze snapped to her face. What he saw there made him stifle a curse.

"Cole? What's happened to Ivan? Tell me," she said in a voice loud enough to cause other diners to glance over at their table.

"Jeez, I'm sorry, Tiffany. I...I thought he told you. Ivan had a little run-in with some men trying to rob his client at gunpoint. That was a week ago."

The color drained from her face. "Oh, my God. Cole, how...how little was little?"

"I swear to you that he wasn't hurt badly, Tiff."

She let out the breath she was holding.

"In fact, I'm shocked that Ivan didn't tell you himself."

"Yeah, me, too," she whispered.

Tiffany's worry soon gave way to anger. "How could he keep information from me like that?"

Cole looked decidedly uncomfortable. "I'm not sure, Tiffany, but I know my brother. His methods may be suspect at times, but I'm confident that Ivan was simply trying to protect you."

She was incredulous. "Protect me?"

"Tiff, it's his job. It's what he does. He puts himself in harm's way to protect others."

"Yeah, well, who the hell protected him, huh? He's supposed to have a team, and his plans are supposed to have backups."

"Tiff, unexpected things happen in the field. Don't worry. Ivan will be okay."

"*This* time, Cole," she said pointedly. "Ivan will be okay this time. But what about next time?"

Two days later, and Tiffany still hadn't heard a word from Ivan. She determined that enough was enough. It was time to get some answers herself. She took a leave of absence and put Celeste in charge, confident that that between her and the other staff, they could handle the shop while she was gone. She told Milán her plan to go to Dubai to see for herself what condition Ivan was in.

"Tiffy, are you sure?"

"What choice do I have? I'm not getting anywhere waiting for him to tell me what happened, and when he did text, he just said he was fine, so yes, I'm going. I need to get a few things straight with Colonel Mangum, and that's better accomplished in person. Since Cole let it leak that he's been injured, how do I know that he even told Cole the full truth? Maybe it's more severe than even he knows. I won't feel better until I can see him face-to-face—to know for myself that he's on the mend."

"I don't know about this. I'd feel more comfortable if Adrian and I went with you."

She hugged her best friend. "I know, Lani, and thank you, but I'll be fine. This is something I have to do on my own. I won't be babied by Ivan or anyone else. It's time he found out that there's no *I* in team."

Chapter 20

There was an intruder at her door. Tiffany was in the middle of packing her passport and other travel documents when she heard a thump from the other room. She glanced at the clock on her nightstand. It was too late to be Milán, and she had just seen her an hour ago. Her heart started pounding in her chest. *She had to do something!*

Silently, Tiffany grabbed her cell phone out of her purse. She crept over to her dresser and opened the top drawer. She took out the Taser that Ivan had given her. She hadn't told him, but she had practiced several times with it, and she knew how to use it. She got it ready to fire, and then stealthily made her way out of her bedroom.

She eased along the walls, ready to defend herself. When she saw her door open, she raised the weapon and took aim.

When she saw Ivan, Tiffany cried out and dropped the Taser and her phone. She bolted across the room and threw herself into his arms.

"Ivan," she exclaimed. "What are you doing here? You're supposed to be in Dubai."

She searched his face, and frowned when she saw the numerous cuts and bruises splattered along the planes of his jaw, as well as the butterfly Band-Aid over his right eye. There were dark circles under his eyes, and his face was transitioning between a five-o'clock shadow and a full-grown beard.

Her hand went to her mouth. "Ivan," she breathed. "My God."

"It's okay," he said tiredly. "I look worse than I feel. At least I do now."

"Good." She helped him over to the couch. Her shock and concern at seeing him were suddenly replaced with anger. When he sat down, she sat next to him and punched him in the arm.

"Ow."

She pointed a finger into his chest. "How could you do this to me, Ivan?"

He stared at her. "Do what?"

"Withhold information." She got up and put some distance between them. He was too close, and she needed to get everything eating away at her out in the open before she caved.

"You were hurt—and from the looks of it, badly. You didn't think that warranted a phone call to let me know what happened? I've been trying to reach you for days, Ivan. Days!" she yelled. "I had no idea where you were, what was happening, or if you were…" Tiffany stopped. She couldn't put a voice to what she had feared above all else.

"This was a complete contradiction to how we're supposed to function. We're a team, Ivan. A team. It's not just about you anymore, remember? You have a responsibility to me, and I to you."

"Tiff, I'm sorry. I just didn't want you worrying about

my condition when I was so far away and there wasn't anything you could do."

"That's not your call to make, Ivan. I deserve to know if something happens to you. I should also have the right to decide if I'm going to come wherever you are to be with you. It doesn't matter how far away you are, I'd be on the first plane to Kathmandu if you needed me. It doesn't matter, Ivan. I'd worry about you whether you were two inches away, or two million," she said, using his words.

"But I'm fine, Tiffany. I'm on the mend so there's no need to worry about me."

Her mouth dropped open, and she stared at him. Without another word, Tiffany walked away from him. She strode into the bedroom, retrieving her cell phone and Taser off the floor, and paced back and forth. Her skin felt like it was on fire, and her breath shuddered from her body as though she'd just run a marathon. Tiffany could not remember the last time she had been this angry.

She heard a knock on the door. "Tiffany, open up."

"I don't want to see you right now, Ivan. I'm too mad, and I'll only say something I'll regret later, so just leave me alone."

"Leave you alone? I flew over seven thousand miles to see you, and now you want me to leave you alone?"

Something in his tone set her off even more. She stomped to the door, unlocked it and flung it open.

"Maybe you should have called first."

He ran a hand over his bearded jaw. "Tiffany, you're right. I'm sorry. I truly am. At the time I was only concerned about you worrying about me and there being nothing you can do. Involving you at that point had no upside."

She pushed past him and strode toward the front door. She held it open and waited.

"What are you doing?" he said from behind her.

"I'll see you later, Ivan. It's obvious we're just going in

circles, and quite frankly, I'm exhausted. I think we need to regroup later."

Ivan stood there. "Are you serious right now?"

"Have you heard a word I've said since you arrived?"

A muscle ticked in Ivan's jaw. "Maybe you're right. This wasn't the reunion either of us was hoping for. We both need to get some sleep and regroup in the morning. I'll call you tomorrow, okay?"

"Fine."

"Good night, Tiffany," he said, and then strode past her.

Tiffany slammed the door. Seconds later, she backed up. She was so angry, she was shaking. Unable to sit still any longer, Tiffany went to grab her purse and car keys. She hit the lights and left without a backward glance. She needed to blow off some steam, and sitting around crying wasn't cutting it.

Ivan sat up in his bed. The movement caused him to grit his teeth. He was in pain, but wasn't about to take the medication a doctor had prescribed. He felt like crap, but he would deal with it. After a restless night, and replaying his conversation with Tiffany in his head, he had to admit that he had handled the situation badly.

"Dude, you look like you've been stomped on and left for dead."

Ivan glanced up to see his brother walking into his bedroom.

"Thanks."

"Don't get me wrong, I'm happy to see you, but why are you here? I thought you went to Tiffany's last night." Cole looked over at the closed bathroom door. "Am I interrupting?"

"No. Tiffany's not here. I came home last night."

"Uh…why?"

"We had a disagreement," Ivan ground out. "I don't

know what the hell happened. One minute we were happy, and the next she was railing on me for not telling her about getting hurt."

"Can you blame her?" Cole reasoned. "Ivan, you should've seen Tiffany's face when I let it slip that you'd been hurt. She was floored."

Ivan sighed heavily. "I know. I just didn't want to worry her. I figured I'd tell her about it when I got here. There was nothing she could do about it, and I was on the mend."

"I don't think that was her point, big brother."

"I know."

"This is her first time dealing with your crazy schedule, Ivan. Her worst fears are realized when she finds out you've been hurt, and then you tell her it's none of her business?"

"I didn't say it like that. I was there and she was here, and I didn't want her worrying needlessly, Cole."

"Look, all I'm saying is that your family is used to how you operate, and the demands of your career. Your girlfriend," he stressed, "is not."

Ivan was thoughtful. Finally he said, "I get it." He nodded at Cole. "Thanks."

"You're welcome. Now, I suggest you try to get some sleep, then take a long shower, a much-needed shave, and get your head on straight before you see Tiffany again. No offense, big brother, but you look kinda shabby."

"Okay, I've let you brood. Now do you want to talk about it?"

Tiffany gazed out over Lake Michigan from her vantage point at Navy Pier. She thought surrounding herself with lots of laughter and excitement would ease the hurt and pain she still felt, but she was wrong. Her disappointment had grown over the past day and still remained front and center in her mind.

"What's the point?" she said woodenly. "Is that going to make Ivan any different? Will it change me?"

"Tiff, this blowup between you just happened yesterday. It's raw, and it's still new. You have to talk it out. That's the only way you'll get past it," Milán reasoned.

"Until when? The next time we have a huge argument? I can't believe he said my feelings didn't matter. Like I don't have the right to be concerned about his life. He's got it all under control. I couldn't possibly understand, or help, or add value to his life. If that's the case, what am I doing in it?"

"Sweetie, you know he didn't say that."

"He might as well have." Tiffany swiped angrily at her tears. "I was stupid to think it could work—that *we* could work."

"Okay, now you're just being silly. You two are great to-gether. Sure, you've had a fight, but all couples do, Tiffany. It's not the end of the world. You'll get past it."

"I'm not being silly, I'm being realistic. He doesn't need anything, or anybody. I'm supposed to just sit back and watch him get hurt, or worse, and not have an opinion or believe that it was all because he wanted to protect me? Like I'm some porcelain doll that will shatter into pieces if handled too roughly? Well, I'm sorry, that doesn't work for me."

Her cell phone chirped. Tiffany reached into her purse and retrieved it. She took one look at the screen and put it back.

"That's Ivan, right?"

She simply nodded.

"Tiff, it's the sixth time he's called since we've been here. How many more from last night and this morning? It's obvious that he's trying to reach you to make things right. Why won't you hear him out?"

"What's left to say? I was about to turn my life upside

down and fly halfway around the world because I was worried to death about him, Lani. And for what? So he can make it seem like I was the one overreacting? He buys me a Taser, gives me self-defense lessons and practically checks under couches in my apartment for burglars to make sure *I'm* safe, but I'm not supposed to care about his safety?"

Her phone chirped again. She snatched it up and turned the power off.

"Tiffany—"

"Forget it. I'm going to work. At least that will take my mind off this whole sordid mess. Ivan coming home was all I could think about for weeks now, but—"

"Focus on that," Milán interjected. "I promise you everything else will work itself out."

Tiffany hugged her best friend, but refrained from comment.

Ivan sat in his truck outside of Tiffany's apartment building, at a complete loss for what to do next. He'd called her cell and work number countless times with no success. He'd even broken down and called Norma Jean, hoping to find her there, but the only thing she had offered was a stern lecture on the stupidity of men. Ivan was in no mood, and ended the call the moment he could interject a word in the middle of her tirade.

Yes, I messed up, but I'm not letting another hour go by before I try to fix it.

Ivan took a few deep breaths and mentally prepared himself for an uphill battle. He would not retreat, no matter the cost. The discord between him and Tiffany could not go on another night. With a determined glint in his eyes, Ivan got out and strode into the building with purposeful steps. He was prepared to do whatever it took to fix the fracture in his relationship with Tiffany. Failure was completely unacceptable.

When he reached her door, he knocked firmly and waited. It was the second time that week he'd found himself on the wrong side of one. He could almost sense the moment Tiffany came up to the peephole, looked out and tried to decide if she would let him in. He was not taking any chances.

"Tiffany, please open the door. I'd really like to talk to you."

Silence.

"A few minutes is all I ask. After that, I'll leave if you want me to."

Painful seconds ticked by, and then she was standing in front of him. Relief washed through him. She stepped aside, allowing him to enter.

"Have a seat."

Ivan lowered himself to the couch, but sat right on the edge as though unable to relax. Tiffany sat across from him. His gazed missed nothing. She looked fatigued, her eyes red and puffy, and she appeared as miserable as he felt. His stomach tightened.

"I understand why you wouldn't take my calls or see me. I appreciate your making an exception this time."

She nodded.

He decided to plunge right in. "I'm sorry I hurt you, Tiffany. I shouldn't have kept you in the dark about what happened. I only wanted to protect you from worrying about me. But I see now that wasn't the best way to handle it."

"No, it wasn't," she replied. "But maybe it was your way of telling me that now isn't the best time for us to be in a relationship. Maybe the last thing you want or need right now is a girlfriend."

Ivan was stunned. "I'm not letting you run away at the first sign of trouble. Relationships take work, Tiffany. We've both got issues to own up to and deal with. If you think I'm throwing in the towel because of one fight, think again."

She jumped to her feet. "One fight? You told me caring about you wasn't my business," she accused.

"That's not what I meant. I merely wanted to keep you from worrying about me from seven thousand miles away. I didn't want to upset you."

"Upset me? So you thought you'd wait until you were right in front of me to kick me in the teeth? Gee, thanks."

"It wasn't like that."

"Then how was it? Tell me, Ivan. I want to know, because just saying you did it for my own good isn't cutting it. It was selfish, inconsiderate and just plain uncaring for you to keep me in the dark about what happened to you."

"I thought it was better that way."

"Why?"

"Because it was bad news."

Tiffany looked confused. "What does that matter?"

"The last long-distance relationship I was in imploded, and it wasn't just because of the infidelity. She…she wasn't good at hearing bad news. She said it was nerve-racking and stressful for her to hear when I'd been injured. So I stopped mentioning it. And there was no way I wanted to take the chance of it happening again. I can't lose you, Tiffany," he said with despair.

"Ivan, I'm not Debra. I want to know and hear everything that goes on with you. Do you know how hurt I felt knowing that you hadn't been honest with me? That you told Cole what happened and not me? It broke my heart. I love you, Ivan, and the thought of losing you was only worsened by the fact that I wouldn't even have known it."

She was crying in earnest now. Ivan walked over and tried to wipe her tears, but she turned away from him.

"Don't."

Ultimately, Tiffany allowed him to comfort her. He

picked her up and set her on the couch in his lap. He held her while she cried.

"God, sweetheart, please don't cry. It's killing me inside. I'm sorry, I just got used to keeping the negative stuff to myself to keep the peace."

"Don't ever keep me in the dark about your safety again. I don't care what happened in the past. I'm not *her*. I don't want that kind of relationship with you, Ivan."

"Okay. No more withholding information."

"You'd better not, or I promise I'll put you in the hospital myself."

"Roger that." He grinned and kissed the top of her head. He held her for a few minutes before he spoke again. "Did you say that you loved me?"

"I don't know," she groused.

She missed the delight in his face. He continued to stroke her back. Suddenly, he stopped. "I noticed luggage in the foyer the night I got back. Where were you going?"

She sighed raggedly. "I was on my way to you."

"What?"

She pushed away from him. "I couldn't stand being without you anymore, Ivan. I know I said I would wait for you here, but then I started to think that I have the means to take off for a while, and that I could be with you in Dubai so that we wouldn't have to be apart."

"Sweetheart, I'm...I'm blown away you'd have done that for me."

"Not just for you. For both of us."

"So you don't want to break up with me anymore?"

"I never did. I was just angry. And you're right. We both have issues to own up to. My track record on relationships is just as spotty as yours, and I did wonder if ending it would've been easier."

He stroked her cheek. "But not anymore?"

She shook her head. "Maybe easier, but I could never do it."

Ivan smiled. "Why?"

"Because I love you too damn much—I have for a long time."

"That's good, because I love you too damn much to ever let you go."

They sealed their new declaration with a kiss. Over her tirade, Tiffany hugged him.

"I'm glad you tried again."

"You're worth it. So how should we celebrate my home-coming and an end to our skirmish—dinner, dancing, a movie? Making love right here, right now?"

"Unless you're hungry, we can order in...later," Tiffany told him. "Right now I want you all to myself."

He kissed her neck. "I can handle that."

Tiffany led him into her bedroom. She made quick work of undressing him. After his pants were gone, she unbuttoned his shirt. When she slid it off, she gasped at seeing the discoloration on his chest and ribs.

"I'm okay," he said quickly. "Completely on the mend."

Tiffany pointed to the bed. "Get in."

She sat cross-legged on the bed and inspected his wounds. "Tell me everything."

He relayed the story of how they got ambushed and the attempted burglary that ensued. "None of us sustained serious harm. Our client and my employees," he clarified. "I didn't care that we knocked around the bad guys pretty good."

"Did you break your ribs?"

"No, just bruised. I fell down a flight of stairs." He grinned. "Well...more like jumped."

She swallowed hard. "Jumped?"

"Yes, one of the perpetrators was getting away. Don't worry, he broke my fall."

"Do not try to make me laugh right now," she cautioned. "I'm still a little mad at you."

His hand slid under her T-shirt. "How mad?"

"Go to sleep, Ivan," she commanded. "You look like you haven't slept in days."

"So do you. Come here."

Tiffany climbed in next to him. She entwined her fingers with his. Seconds later, they were both sound asleep.

Chapter 21

Ivan asleep past eight in the morning just wasn't heard of. Tiffany was shocked. That had never happened since she had known him. Not once.

She tried not to make a lot of noise as she left the room so that he could get the rest his body needed.

After eating, Tiffany fell asleep on the living room couch. When Ivan stood over her, his presence awoke her. She blinked a few times. "Hi," she said sleepily.

"Hey, baby."

"I was trying not to wake you. I must've dozed off." She sat up.

"I don't blame you. It's been a stressful few days."

"Try few months, but not nearly as bad as yours."

He held his hand out to her. "I have an idea. Let's spend the rest of the day in bed. We'll be bed potatoes."

Tiffany's eyebrows went upward. "Bed potatoes?" She got up. "Have you ever done that before?"

His smile was infectious, and Tiffany couldn't help being caught up in the bizarre proposition.

"Probably not, but for you, I'll make an exception."

It was surprising to both of them how committed they were to doing nothing. They napped, talked, watched a movie and then napped again. Later, Tiffany ordered food to be delivered. After eating, they went back to sleep.

When Tiffany awoke again, it was to find Ivan hovering over her with a breakfast tray. She sat up and eyed the generous helpings of croissants, bacon, eggs and fruit.

"All this was in my kitchen?"

"No." He laughed. "It was pretty lean in there."

He sat next to her and read the paper while they ate.

"What do you want to do today?" she inquired between bites.

"We should swing past my house so I can go through all the mail and do a few other menial tasks—you know, go to the dry cleaner's, wash clothes, make love to my girl."

"Oh, that," she dismissed. "It all sounds so mundane." She yawned for effect. "How do you stand it?"

He tweaked her nose. "We all have our jobs to do. Tonight, though, is all yours. We're getting dressed up, and we're going out to dinner."

Tiffany perked up. "Really?"

"Yep, and I have a gift for you. It's in the living room."

When she returned, she was lugging a big square box. "Ivan, I didn't see this last night. I'm sure I would've remembered."

"It was in the car."

She untied the huge bow and took the top off. Under several layers of tissue paper was a stunning gown. "Ivan," she breathed, and then got up to hold the dress out in front of her. "Oh, my God, you brought me a Donna Karan gown?"

Tiffany stared at the cross-neck, claret-colored, full-length jersey gown. It was slinky, sexy and elegant. "I'm… Wow…I don't know what to say. Thank you."

"I thought we'd do it up tonight. You deserve it, sweetheart. There's something else in the box, too."

She went back and searched until she found an envelope. She opened it.

"A day at the spa?"

"You got it. A full body massage, facial treatment, manicure, pedicure, hair and makeup."

A gleam of pleasure covered her face. "But…you said we had laundry and house stuff to do."

"I have laundry and house stuff," he corrected. "You, my darling, have a day of other people catering to your needs. Don't worry, I'll take up my shift tonight." He winked.

She set the gown back in its box and placed it in her walk-in closet. She returned, and as gently as she could, jumped into his arms. Ivan caught her and rubbed his hands up and down her back.

"Are you happy?"

"Ecstatic," she confirmed. "But you didn't have to do all this just because we had a fight."

"I have a confession. All this was planned prior to the battle." His fingers traced the outline of her lower lip. "Do you love me?"

Her eyes lit up with happiness. "Yes, Ivan Mangum. I love you."

Ivan allowed his happiness to shine through, too. "Say it again."

"I love you."

They kissed, and then she moved off to the side of him. She laid her head on his chest. His heartbeat was loud and steady.

"I love you, too, Tiffany."

She listened to his declaration through his chest. She raised her head. "Say it again."

"I love you, Tiffany Gentry. The time away from you has been torture for me. I couldn't wait to get home and tell you how much I loved you. I want to make sure that I never let you forget just how much."

"Thank you, Ivan. This has been the best night I've ever had."

Ivan kissed her soundly. "For both of us, love."

It didn't take Tiffany long to realize that Ivan had spared no expense in making their evening memorable. He dropped her off at the spa before promising to pick her up later so she could go home and change for dinner.

The only word that came to mind as her day stretched out before her was *decadence.* Her relaxation level increased with each service she received. By the end of the day, Tiffany felt like royalty. Ivan sent a text to head out front. She thanked the staff and slowly walked outside.

There was a stretch limousine at the curb and a man holding up a printed sign with her name. Tiffany smiled and shook her head. *Ivan.*

"I'm Miss Gentry."

"Hello, madam. My name is Smithers, and I will be your driver for this evening."

He was British. Tiffany shook his hand. "Hello, Mr. Smithers."

The driver assisted her inside. She discovered a bottle of chilled champagne that had just been opened, a bowl of fresh strawberries and a single red rose standing regally in a vase next to the ice bucket. She lowered a strawberry into the bubbly and took a sip. Tiffany settled in for the drive to her home, but instead they headed to Lake Shore Drive, and then back through the city. The car pulled to a stop. She peeked out the window. Her mouth gaped open.

Smithers opened her door and escorted her onto the sidewalk, handing her bags to a waiting porter. "Welcome to

the Trump International Hotel and Tower, Miss Gentry."
He handed her an envelope. "I'll see you shortly."

Tiffany opened the envelope and retrieved a card. "See
you at eight, love I." Her pulse raced with excitement.

She checked in at the front desk and was escorted upstairs. From the moment Tiffany stepped over the threshold
of her room, she was in the lap of luxury. Ivan had reserved
a one-bedroom suite with a scenic view of the river. It was
eleven hundred square feet of pure indulgence. A large flat-
panel television sat on a low table. There was a fireplace, a
plush couch and chair with an ottoman, a kitchenette with
granite countertops, stainless-steel appliances and a dining table and chairs.

She moved to the bedroom. A king-size bed sat regally
in the middle of the room with a floor-to-ceiling wood
headboard. The furnishings were muted colors in gray,
taupe and white. The view of the city was stunning. The
en-suite bathroom was like a personal spa with rich neutral
tiles, a chocolate wood table with glass sink bowls, fluffy
white towels and thick terry-cloth bathrobes.

"Unbelievable." Before she could say another word, a
light knock sounded at her door.

She went to open it. Two women with carry-on bags
greeted her.

"May I help you?"

"Miss Gentry?"

"Yes."

"Hi, we're your hair and makeup stylists for tonight."

"Oh. Come in," she said, stepping aside.

Ivan had pulled out all the stops on the day just for her,
and she was going to ensure that he received his money's
worth. By the time he saw her that evening, she would be
as primped and coiffed as she could possibly be.

After a delectable bath prepared by one of her stylists,
Tiffany submerged herself up to her neck in rich, perfumed

water infused with rose petals. It was straight out of a movie. She couldn't wait to tell Milán and Jeannie about her lavish day.

By the time she was completely dressed and ready two hours later, she felt like Julia Roberts in *Pretty Woman*. Except Richard Gere wasn't the one waiting for her in the hotel lobby—it was Ivan standing in front of the limo dressed in a black shawl collar dinner suit. His tall, well-built physique definitely did his attire justice. He was clean-shaven and too desirable for her to put into words. She tried, but the only thing that escaped her lips came out in a soft whisper. "Have mercy."

When she reached him, Ivan's eyes roamed over her wine-colored gown, her smoothed hair and plum-tinted lips. Lips that, if he were lucky, would travel all over his body later. The thought made him grin. Ivan held out his hand when she reached him. Her fingers lightly touched his before he raised his hand up and slowly rotated her around. Her hair was slicked down and reminiscent of old Hollywood glamour. The only ornamentation was a single diamond pin. The style accented the low-dipped back of her gown.

When he completed the turn, he raised her hand up to his lips. "Have mercy, indeed."

Her eyes widened in surprise. "You read lips, too?"

"Only yours," he remarked smoothly.

Ivan took her wrap and helped her into the limousine. Smithers shut the door behind them. Before their driver pulled off, he raised the privacy shield between them.

Tiffany turned to Ivan. "Do you know how ridiculously pampered I felt today…right now? Ivan, no one has ever, ever spoiled me this way before. It wasn't just about the money you spent, it was the thought and love that went into it. Those simple gestures were loud and clear amidst all the extravagance. I just wanted you to know that I saw them, and they mattered."

"Tiffany, you are such an exceptional woman—you're kind, thoughtful, sexy as hell, smart, determined and loyal to those you love. I would spoil you like this each day if I thought you'd let me."

"I hope you know you've exceeded all my expectations tonight."

He held up her hand and kissed a trail down her arm. His eyes glittered like a tiger stalking his prey. "Lord, I hope not. Then again, there are plenty of hours left for you to have a change of heart."

Tiffany reveled in the moment…their moment.

By the time they returned to the hotel, Tiffany had been thoroughly wined and dined. As they rode the elevator up to their suite, she looked to him and said, "You've definitely made up for not telling me about getting hurt. In case there was any doubt, you're forgiven."

He opened the door for her. "Well, if I wasn't, I think I have just the thing that would've sealed the deal."

Tiffany walked through the door and stopped in her tracks. The living room had been transformed with music, a fire and lit candles. On the dining table there was another bottle of champagne with a platter of fruits dipped in chocolate.

"I know what you're thinking. You're thinking that I'm the most romantic man you've ever met."

She peeped up at him from under her eyelashes. "Yes, but I guarantee that is *not* what I was thinking."

"Ah. My mind-reading skills aren't what they used to be." He held out his hand. "Would you care to dance, Miss Gentry?"

"I'd love to, Colonel Mangum."

Ivan twirled her into the center of the room, and then they swayed in time to Smokey Robinson's "Cruisin'."

"I love it when we're cruisin' together," he sang in her ear.

"He sings, and dances, too. Is there anything you can't do?" she said as he dipped her.

"There are most definitely a few things on that list, but luckily for you, romancing my woman ain't one of them."

"I love it, I love it, I love it, I love it…" she sang back.

Ivan smiled. "Oh, my lady also has a few hidden talents. Can't wait to see what else you have in your bag of tricks."

When the song ended, Ivan went to pour two glasses of Dom Pérignon. He handed one to Tiffany before unbuttoning his jacket and taking it off. He laid it across a dining room chair.

"Did I mention how incredibly hot you look in that suit? All the women stared when we came in just now. That must happen in a lot of places you go, doesn't it? London, Venice, Dubai…"

Ivan set his glass down on the table. He sauntered over to Tiffany. He slid a finger down her bare arm. "I only have eyes for one woman. Anything else is a job hazard."

Tiffany heard the words, and the solemn way he said them.

"There were a fair share of men ogling you tonight, too. I should've set up a fail-safe on your security system to alert me when a man's checking out your delectable backside."

She heard the same hint of jealousy in his voice that had been in hers. "I only have eyes for one man. Anything else is a job hazard."

Ivan wrapped his arms around her waist and hoisted her up so they were at eye level. "That's good to know, because I don't play nice with my toys."

She felt pure satisfaction at his possessive words. Tiffany kissed him. "You're the only man who's ever getting my toys."

Ivan carried her into the bedroom. It was laid out in a

similar fashion with only candles illuminating in the room. He stopped at the bed, but did not set her down.

"I'd like to seal our pledge of fidelity with a kiss, but I think I can go one better than that."

He placed her on the bed and retrieved a bag from the dresser. He took out a light blue box with a white bow and placed it in her lap. She gazed at the signature wrapping.

"Tiffany?"

"A Tiffany for my Tiffany." Suddenly, Ivan burst out laughing. "Okay, who would've thought I'd ever get to say that?"

She laughed, too, then untied the box and opened it. Her fingers trembled as she held the small package suspended in midair.

"Ivan…it's an engagement ring," she choked out.

"Yes, it is. A one-carat Tiffany Novo, to be exact, but only if you let me put it on your finger. That's the engagement part. If not, it's just a brilliant ring in a box."

The tears welled up in her eyes. She gawked at him. "Really?"

He took the ring from the box, and then took her hand. "I could give you thousands of reasons why I want you to spend the rest of your life by my side, but the truth is, Tiffany Adele Gentry, the most important one is that I simply—" his voice faltered "—love you, and can't live without you anymore. The time we were apart truly put things in perspective for me. You're everything to me, and I want you by my side—always. So will you do me the greatest honor of becoming my wife?"

"Yes, Ivan Thomas Mangum," she said simply. "Yes, I'll marry you…because I love you and can't be without you, either."

He kissed her left hand before sliding the diamond ring onto her third finger.

"It fits perfectly—just like we do."

"We just got engaged." She sniffed. "We're getting married."

"You got that right." Ivan pulled her into his lap. The fabric from her gown pooled around them.

Tiffany took his head in her hands. "I love you, Ivan Mangum. I always have."

"You'd better, Tiffany soon-to-be Mangum, or this would have been the most expensive date I've ever had."

"Ivan?"

"Yes, my lovely fiancée?"

"Make love to me."

He laid her down on the bed. His hand lightly caressed her cheek before moving lower. "I've wanted to do nothing else since the first day I met you."

Time ceased to matter outside of their illuminated piece of paradise. Ivan carefully removed her gown, and Tiffany helped him out of his suit.

She backed up and climbed onto the bed. She held out a finger and beckoned him over. "You did say you wanted to see what was in my bag of tricks."

In an instant, Ivan was on the bed and kissing a trail up her body. His eyes glowed with excitement. "Bring the rain, baby."

"I can't stop staring at it," she gushed the next morning. "My ring is so beautiful."

"We should definitely throw an engagement party the next time I'm home."

"I agree."

"Do you think we need an event planner?"

The look she gave him spoke volumes. He chuckled. "Okay, that's a no."

"This is our engagement and our wedding. I want us to experience these once-in-a-lifetime moments as much as possible."

He squeezed her hand. "However you want to do this is one hundred percent fine with me. My time and my credit card are at your disposal."

"Ivan, you don't have to do that."

He glanced over. "True, but I'm doing it. My grandmother alone can drink enough Grey Goose to put the bartender's kids through college."

Tiffany giggled. "She does not."

"I'm telling you, she was on her good behavior at my going-away party. She could've drunk us all under the table."

Early that afternoon, Smithers returned to pick them up. In the car, Tiffany fell asleep with her left hand resting on Ivan's thigh. Even through his jeans, he could pinpoint every inch of skin that connected with his leg. He got turned on just thinking about the ways he was going to bring her body to ecstasy.

"Tiffany?" he said urgently.

"Hmm?" She opened her eyes. "Are we there yet?"

There was a gleam in his eye when he reached over and kissed her neck. "Not yet, sweetheart. We're taking a minor detour."

She sat up. "We are? Why?"

"Smithers," Ivan called out.

"Yes, sir?"

Ivan glanced down at his bride-to-be. "We'll be taking the long way home."

"Very good, sir."

Tiffany blushed profusely as the privacy glass slid up between them.

"Do you think we'll ever make it anywhere without taking a…detour?"

"I think you need to be concerned when we don't want to take a detour," he said with a wink.

* * *

That night, a thunderstorm rolled in. There was a crack of lightning, and a loud clap of thunder shook the house. Tiffany sat up with a jolt.

"Ivan," she called.

"Right here, sweetheart." He rushed to her side.

Tiffany wrapped her arms around him. "Where were you?"

"Just looking at the storm. Hey, what's wrong?"

"You were gone. You didn't come home when you said you would, and then I'm in some strange place looking for you, and I can't find you. I'm looking everywhere, and each face looks the same. I can't speak the language, and then I see you and you're working, but then you turn to come help me and you get hurt, Ivan. I—"

"Shh, it was just a dream, Tiff. You're safe, and so am I. I'm here, sweetheart. We're in my bed. Can you feel me?"

She hugged him tighter, afraid to break contact with him in case he was an illusion. She let out a shuddering sigh. "Yes."

Ivan stretched out on the bed next to her. He rubbed Tiffany's back in circles hoping to calm her down. After a few minutes, her breathing evened out.

"I'm sorry."

"For what? Having a nightmare?"

She put her arms under her head to prop herself up on his chest. "Yes. I don't want to worry you...not before you go. You need to be focused on your work, not me. I don't want you thinking I can't handle you being gone, because I can, and I'll never be untrue to you, Ivan. I'll be a good wife."

He ran his fingers through her hair. "I know you will, Tiff." He sat up. "Hey, where's all this coming from?"

"I've never done this before, and none of my relationships lasted. My parents were miserable, but I don't want you worrying about me when you're out there doing your job, okay? Your safety is what's most important. I don't ever want to be a distraction," she finished in a rush.

"You aren't," he assured her. "You'll be on my mind wherever I am, sweetheart, but I don't have any doubts about your abilities, Tiffany. You're strong, capable and loyal. I know you'll always protect me and the family that we create together. You'll be a fantastic wife and mother. Sweetheart, loving you is never, ever a distraction for me. It's a blessing to me. You're not jeopardizing my job by becoming my wife, Tiffany. If anything, you're keeping me safer, because I have someone at home who loves me and needs me to return. You keep me grounded—and focused." He tilted her face upward so that they made eye contact. "Never doubt that, okay?"

Too emotional to speak, Tiffany could only nod. Ivan held her until she fell back asleep.

"Come on, sleepyhead, breakfast is ready."

Ivan rolled over. His head was pounding, and he felt like he'd been jumped on in the middle of the night and thrown back into bed. He sat up and observed his awake and extremely chipper fiancée.

"Good morning," he said hoarsely. "Why are you up so early?"

"It's actually not that early," she informed him. "It's ten."

"Ten?" Ivan sat up, fully alert. "What is going on with me? I'm usually not a late sleeper."

"You should be when you can. You don't sleep nearly as much as you should."

"Years and years of painful memories," he answered honestly. "Some things stay with you."

Sitting on the bed, Tiffany handed him a tray. A look of understanding dawned on her face. "I get it. I'm sorry, Ivan."

"Don't be sorry, Tiffany. I did the job that I had to do—and still do. I'm living my dream every day. A few lost hours of sleep are a small price to pay to keep people safe." He folded a large amount of pancakes into his mouth. He sighed. "Wow, these are incredible."

"I'm glad you like them. It's my grandmother's recipe."

He nodded. "These are awesome. When you create one, make sure that recipe is in *our* family cookbook."

She beamed. "I will."

"There's one thing today that's pretty important that we need to take care of."

"What?"

"We haven't set our date yet."

Six weeks later...

"I think December 24 is a perfect day for a wedding," Norma Jean gushed to Ivan's grandmother at Tiffany and Ivan's engagement party. "Of course, that doesn't give them much time to plan a wedding, but I'm sure it will go off without a hitch. Ivan is everything I want for Tiffany and more. I couldn't be happier. Besides Adrian and Milán, they're my best match."

"Your match? The way Ivan tells it, you kept fixing Tiffany up with men who were completely unsuitable for her, and that they got together on their own."

Norma Jean sat down next to Cecile. "You know, sometimes getting a basket full of prepackaged fruit isn't what it's cracked up to be. On the top, you might have some good-looking fruit that's shiny and appealing, but if you buy the whole basket without delving deeper, you might find yourself at home later with some old, rotten pieces, too. But when you pick and choose the fruit yourself, taking the time to really look around, you find the fruit that you were meant to have. That's the kind that tastes the sweetest."

Cecile snorted. "Are you saying you planted my grandson in Tiffany's fruit basket?"

Norma Jean smiled. "I'm saying that things have worked out the way they were meant to."

"Well, it's all kind of fast, don't you think? Don't get me wrong, I love Tiffany. She's time enough for my grandson, but in my day we had courtships. Weddings took time to plan, and there was a great deal to do." Cecile observed Tiffany and Ivan from across the room.

"Kids nowadays rush to do everything," Norma Jean agreed. "But in this case, they truly love each other and can't wait to start their lives together. With Ivan traveling as much as he does, I think they should cut the long engagement short. Besides, I think it's much more romantic than an extended, drawn-out affair."

A round of toasts was done by Norma Jean and Heathcliffe, Cole, Milán and Adrian, and lastly, Ivan's grandmother.

Next Tiffany presented Ivan with a gift. He opened the box and held up a charm of two white-gold swans interlocked to form one heart.

"Sweetheart, it's beautiful."

"This is so you'll always remember how strong our love is," she explained. "Like this symbol, we're joined together by love, faith and commitment. You're taking my heart with you to Dubai, Ivan. I won't be whole again until you return."

He swept her up into his arms and kissed her. "I love you," he whispered for her ears only.

"I love you," she whispered back.

He held out a beautifully decorated box. She opened the gift to find a date book with a bright red piece of fabric.

She went to that page and flipped it open. Each box had a red X across the date. She turned to the next calendar, and it was the same. She flipped through the remainder of the calendar until it ended. Curious, she gazed up at Ivan.

"When I come back next week, I'm not going on any assignments again until after we're married and back from our honeymoon."

Tiffany's face lit up. "Ivan, are you serious? I'll have you all to myself till the end of January?"

He nodded. "At least. Can you handle that, Mrs. Mangum-to-be?"

She wrapped her arms around his neck and kissed him soundly. "You know, I think I could definitely get used to that."

She loved this man so much. There may be obstacles to face on the road ahead, but they would face them together. Ivan always said that they did their best work together, and it was true. He had done much more than protect her since walking through her door months before. He had restored her faith in love, in the commitment between a man and a woman, and the notion that there was truly a happily-ever-after. Ivan Mangum was all she had ever wanted. She had found her heart's desire.

Epilogue

The marriage of Colonel Ivan Thomas Mangum to Tiffany Adele Gentry was a very grand affair. They were married at Ivan's parents' church in Beverly, followed by an elegant reception at the Trump International Hotel and Tower, where the newlywed couple truly started their amazing journey together. The bride wore a Vera Wang gown, and the groom a black Brioni tuxedo.

Several hours later, the groom carried his bride upstairs to the same suite they'd used the night Ivan proposed. The next day, they would fly to the exotic retreat of Turtle Island in Fiji and stay in an ultraprivate villa called a *bure* that overlooked the Blue Lagoon. The pictures looked breathtaking, and Tiffany couldn't wait to get there and be totally alone with her new husband.

Ivan was lying on their bed wearing only silk pajama bottoms. His arms were crossed behind his head, patiently waiting for his bride to emerge from the bathroom.

"Should I send in the troops?" he called out.

"I don't think you want them seeing your wife like this," she replied sweetly.

Moments later, Tiffany appeared in a long silk gown. It curved around her body like a second skin before trailing behind her.

"Wow," Ivan said appreciatively. "You were most definitely worth the wait." He held his hand out. "Come here, Mrs. Mangum."

She walked over slowly so that she could afford him a longer view. She stopped at the edge of the bed. He stood up and took her hand to ceremoniously spin her around to see the back of her gown. He was not disappointed at seeing the now signature plunging back.

"You're a vision," he said reverently.

"Today is the most perfect day of my life," she said tearfully.

He captured a tear between his thumb and forefinger. "There'll be plenty more, I promise."

"Yes, but only one wedding night."

"That will most assuredly be true for you because I'm not letting you go…ever," Ivan pledged.

She stood on her tiptoes and kissed him.

"Would you like your gift now, Mrs. Mangum?"

Tiffany glanced down at her ring finger. In addition to her diamond engagement ring, there was now a one carat wedding band of cognac and white diamonds. They reminded her of her husband's eyes. She was blissfully happy. "I'll never tire of hearing you call me that," she confessed.

"I'll never tire of saying it." His kissed her again before walking around the bed to the nightstand. He opened the drawer and pulled out a small box.

"That was there the whole time?"

"Yep. Hey, I can't help it if you're not that inquisitive."

"Wait," she said and then went to pull a box of her own out of her purse. "I've got a gift for you, too."

"Open mine first," he instructed, before handing it to her.

Tiffany scooted to the middle of the bed. Ivan joined her. She sat cross-legged and opened the box. There was a velvet bag inside. She opened it and turned it upside down. A key fell into her palm. She gazed up at Ivan.

"Is this what I think it is?" Tiffany whispered.

"It is. We're now homeowners of a modest cottage in Oak Park."

She threw herself into his arms, laughing and crying simultaneously. "Is it the Mangum version of a cottage?" She laughed.

"Of course." He grinned. "Just under six thousand square feet, and waiting for its mistress to decorate it however she chooses. I've got some pictures, too," he told her excitedly. "We'll move in when we get back from our honeymoon."

"Oh, Ivan," she cried. "I love my wedding gift."

"I'm glad," he said, in a relieved voice. "Because it would've been a bear to return."

"Now it's your turn." Tiffany handed him her gift-wrapped box. Ivan tore into it with excitement.

"Is it a new Audi sports car?"

"Not this time."

"Golf clubs?"

She shook her head. "Nope."

Ivan opened the box and stared at his gift almost a full ten seconds before his startled gaze met his wife's patient one.

"Is this what I think it is?" he said hoarsely.

He held up the sonogram picture. "Tiffany, you're pregnant?"

"Yes," she cried. "That's a picture of Baby Mangum. It's too early to determine if it's a boy or girl yet. And I wouldn't want to know anyway...not without you."

Ivan leaned over and kissed his wife reverently on the lips. "This is the best gift in the world, sweetheart. Thank you." His voice was heavy with emotion. He wiped the tears from her eyes with his thumb.

"I can't take all the credit. You helped."

Ivan stared at his baby's sonogram again. "I'm going to be a daddy." He looked up at her. "When?"

"Our baby will be making his or her grand entrance sometime in July."

Ivan did the calculations. He started to laugh. "I'll bet we created this wonderful little person the night we got engaged."

"In this bed," she mused. "Talk about amazing."

Ivan leaned Tiffany back, and then settled right beside her. He rested his head on his hand. The other one traced a path from her heart to her stomach. "I can't believe we made a baby." He touched her face. "He or she is our engagement and wedding gift."

"You said we work well together," she reminded him.

"Well, the proof of our handiwork is snuggled safe and sound in here," he said, rubbing her stomach.

"Honestly, I'm still in shock. It's hard to process all of the good fortune we've had in such a short amount of time. We found each other, we fell in love…got engaged…got pregnant…"

"And got married—all within a few months."

"Don't forget the cottage we now own."

"Just in time," he said seriously.

"Ivan, our baby isn't going to need all that space."

"Trust me, we'll need it. Once our family and friends find out you're pregnant, they'll be permanent fixtures."

Suddenly recognition dawned on Tiffany's face. She started laughing.

Ivan stared at her. "What?"

Tears of joy trickled down her face. She glanced lovingly at her husband, the man she'd fallen in love with the moment she saw him. Their love was the kind that dreams were made of.

Ivan sat up. "Tiffany, will you please tell me what's going on?"

"Nothing…everything," she exclaimed. "Ivan, I just can't believe our good fortune. I've never been happier in my life."

"Me neither, sweetheart, but I'll need a new charm."

She looked at him questioningly.

"Remember the charm you gave me for my engagement gift? There were two swans entwined as a symbol of our love. Now we'll need three."

* * * * *